RADGEPACKET

Tales from the Inner Cities

Volume Four

A collection of short fiction from around Great Britain.

Featuring

Danny King

Ian Ayris

Keith Gingell

Carol Fenlon

Gareth Mews

Patrick Belshaw

Fiona Glass

Ragna Brent

Philip Clark

Stephen Cooper

Blaine Ward

Ray Banks

Andy Rivers

Callum Mitchell

Craig Douglas

Darren Sant

Paul Brazill

Andrew Kirby

Steve Porter

Jason Williams

Guy Mankowski

Tom Arnold

Published by:-

Byker Books
Banbury
Oxon

www.bykerbooks.co.uk

2010

ISBN 978-0-9560788-5-8

HERE WE ARE AGAIN...

Alreet?

Aye, you're right, we're at it again. Bringing you quality, short, British fiction from the cream of people you haven't yet heard of and some you have.

If you're a regular 'Radgy' (and why wouldn't you be eh!!) you'll find that in this volume we've re-jigged the format a little. You told us what you wanted and we did it. Out have gone the interviews and competitions. In has come more stories, more pages and more renegade writers from the margins of society.

That's not to say we're neglecting your penchant for the odd 'name' writer...oh no. Danny King's back and he's brought Ray Banks with him. Using a bit of publisher muscle (massive they are...massive!) we've managed to persuade rising star Andy Rivers to dip his nib for us an all.

In this book you'll find stories of Burglars, Nutters, Free Spirits, Chavs, Bands and...well...all sorts of casualties and dregs from these fair shores really.

As we may have mentioned before, our books are for adults and if you feel you may be offended by profanity, sexual acts and drug references then you shouldn't read it - obviously you can still buy it, just don't read it....

Ed

HAPPY AS CAN BE....

Contents

Ragna Brent

As a mum of six, and grandmother of two, Ragna thinks it's a miracle that she manages to construct a sentence. Living in Milton Keynes she has finally mastered roundabouts, although her husband may disagree. She was thrilled in 2008/9 to have several stories published in both the USA and UK. She is hoping 2010 will prove to be as successful. One day she will finish her novel.

Piano Man

I wasn't quite sure how long I'd been dead. It's not the sort of thing you really analyse on a day to day basis is it?

'Am I dead today?'

Although some mornings after a particularly heavy night down the 'Red Lion' with the lads, it's the question I do ask.

It wasn't as if I was here one minute and gone to the after-life the next either. For a few surreal moments I was neither here nor there. I'd been walking along Trent Road minding my own business, like you do. The main thoughts running through my mind involved Ruth Connor's breasts rubbing up against me. I think it's only fair to explain that any thoughts I have regarding the female sex are normally day dreams. In my world, Ruth doesn't even know my name, let alone rub any part of her body against me. It's the story of my life. It was the same with Tracey Harris, Beth Hope, Sarah Cross and...well... I think you may be getting the picture. But a guy can dream can't he? I feel it's good for you as a reader to know what kind of sad loser I am. And, from what you are about to read - not just in my love life.

So, where was I? Oh yes, Saturday afternoon in Trent Road. Apart from Ruth's anatomy, I was watching a ruddy great big black cloud in the sky, and wondering if it was about to chuck it down on me, and more importantly my new Armani shirt. I confess, it wasn't really Armani, but it only cost me eight quid from the market and I felt well kushty in it - the business. I was walking past the flats, you know the sort. Four blocks high with the brick balconies. The ones that as soon as you step in the front door you're hit by the aroma of piss, curry, and dogshit. Yeah, I thought you'd know which ones I meant. It was from one of the top balconies I could hear two blokes effing and blinding and I wasn't really taking much notice.

Well, that was until the piano hit me. Yes, an upright fuck-ing piano, I kid you not. I glanced up and there it was heading straight for me. I think my last words were something along the lines of 'What the...' I never even got to the end of the sentence. The noise of it hitting the decks and me was deafening. Then I was dead.

Only I could get killed by a piano. For fuck's sake I couldn't be normal and be knocked down by a hit and run driver. Even a terminal illness seems more appealing. Imagine my mates eating the grapes while my mother holds my hand telling me how much I mean to her. Maybe I would have stood a chance with Ruth then. She'd have been told about poor Paul, and crept into my hospital room in the middle of the night ...no, no that's another filthy daydream. None of that for me, I had to be killed by a musical instrument. My epitaph will no doubt read something along the lines '*RIP Paul Taylor, gave a new meaning to the song Piano Man.*'

I can just hear the lads now, singing the lyrics and taking the piss. Bastards. Next thing I know is that I'm standing next to my body. Well what I could see of it beneath the pile of wood and iron frame. The only things that appeared intact were the black and white keys grinning at me. Wasn't quite the Saturday afternoon I'd been planning if I'm honest. Course I was gutted. Shane had just texted me to tell me he was getting me one in. The pint I never got. Doubt it sat there long either.

Then this bright orange light appeared. Funny what you think, even when you're dead.

'Oh God I'm about to be Tangoed.'

That's when I saw them standing there. Three beautiful birds dressed in white, beckoning me to join them. I looked around, surely they weren't talking to me? I'm not kidding you, they were straight out of Nuts Magazine - fit as. I walked towards them and they all held out their hands pulling me into the light. So like I say, I wasn't quite sure how long I'd been dead, but I'm thinking that I might just get used to this.

<u>Fiona Glass</u>

Fiona lives in a pointy house in Birmingham
with one husband and far too many spiders.
She writes darkly humorous fiction and has
been known to turn people who annoy her
into victims in her stories. You have been
warned! You can find Fiona's work online at
www.fiona-glass.com

Lemon Sour

The glove was right at the back of the drawer - dusty, crumpled, squashed under her mother's sewing box and half a lifetime's collection of handbags and belts. Jenny wouldn't even have found it if she hadn't been hunting high and low for her mother's heart pills, which the old dear had stashed away somewhere '*safe*'. She recognised it the minute her hands touched the leather though, and brought it out between two fingers with an odd little shudder.

For a single glove, it was a potent reminder. A symbol of her childhood and everything that had been wrong with it. It was faded now and the finger pads were grubby where a child's hands had touched things they shouldn't while wearing the gloves. Magazine print, perhaps, or a sticky bag of sweets, or the moss that grew in soft green cushions on top of the garden wall. Below the stains though, and inside the cuffs where the leather hadn't seen the light of day, you could still see the colour it had been. A pale, pretty lemon yellow - the colour of primroses, or kitchen units from the fifties, before Jenny was born. Her grandmother had had a kitchen that colour when Jenny was very small.

'Quickly, dear,' - a wavering croak, and she could hear her mother's breathing, harsh and laboured, from the room next door.

'In a minute, I can't find them,' she called back, thrusting the glove away again and banging drawers open and closed at random. 'Where did you say you'd put them?'

'...back of the drawer,' came the wheezy reply.

Was it just her imagination or was her mother's voice fading the way the yellow leather had faded over the years? It had been crystal-bright originally, with clear diction and the received pronunciation beloved of everyone of a certain age and class. Now it was hoarse and the words were slightly slurred, the product of last year's minor stroke. Jenny still found it odd not hearing the strident tones that had formed such a cut-glass counterpoint to her childhood years.

'*Keeping up one's standards*': that had been a favourite; along with '*doing things properly*' and '*what will the neighbours think*'. Meaningless platitudes, most of them, designed to deflate argument and crush teenage rebellion in its tracks. Jenny had only to hear the words '*Now, dear, we must all keep our standards up,*' and her resolve would fade, no matter how much she wanted to resist. It was impossible to argue with something so woolly and vague.

'I know that, but which one?' she called back. There were three chests of drawers and two cupboards in the guest bedroom - it would take her hours to search each and every one. Time her mother probably didn't have. There was no reply; she would have to do this on her own, and do it fast.

Her mind went back to the gloves, even as she rattled handles and slammed cupboard doors. When was the last time she'd worn them, the last time she'd succumbed to the insidious drip of her mother's voice? Cousin Jack's wedding? A holiday somewhere? No. A hot flush of shame flooded her limbs, even now, nearly thirty years later, as she recalled the time and place. It had been nowhere more exotic than their local high street, one Saturday afternoon. Jenny, aged fourteen and with a teenager's need for independence, had asked to go shopping with her friends. Her mother had refused, saying brightly, 'You can come with me instead. We'll have tea at the Copper Kettle - you know you love their scones. It'll be such a treat.'

In vain Jenny had tried to explain that fourteen-year-olds didn't go shopping with their mothers, and that anyway, she wanted records and cheap jewellery and cosmetics, not to trail round her mother's favourite boutiques. 'It'll be boring,' she'd said, the teenager's unending cry. Her mother dealt swiftly with that, and worse was to come. Casting a critical eye over Jenny's clothes, she'd said 'You can't possibly go out looking like that. Go up and get changed at once. Your lemon suit will do - it's very pretty and it makes you look pretty too.'

'But Mum,' Jenny had said, her heart sinking in the direction of her platform shoes. 'Everyone wears jeans and stuff. I'll look stupid in a suit.'

'Don't be silly, dear. Auntie Di was very generous giving you that suit. The least you can do is show your gratitude by wearing it. And I won't have you going out in jeans. You need to learn to dress nicely.'

Dress nicely... dress nicely... dress nicely.... The words echoed like train wheels on a track all the way upstairs, and the whole time Jenny was getting changed. She dragged on the hated yellow suit, which had a skirt that finished four inches below her knees and a jacket that stopped at her hips, leaving her bum exposed. Under the jacket she wore a blouse her mother had bought, white with broderie anglaise, and she finished off the outfit with ankle socks and her sensible 'good for your feet' shoes. She turned her back to the mirror, knowing she looked like a frump. The suit might have looked good on her aunt, who was thirty-eight and old, but on a girl like herself the lines were all wrong - a throwback to a bygone age. And when her mother insisted she wore the yellow gloves as well, Jenny's nightmare was complete.

She paraded down the high street at her mother's side, tugging at the jacket from time to time and wishing the pavement would eat her up. She felt as though every pair of eyes in town was on her, as though every conversation involved the suit and every laugh was aimed her way. Bad enough that complete strangers should see her looking like this, but her mortification increased tenfold when they walked out of a fur-coat shop and straight into a gaggle of her friends. There were half a dozen or more, kicking around outside the local café with bottles of coke in their hands: Mary and Suzanne and Gillian from school, and Gillian's best friend Pam, and some other girls she didn't know. On the fringes of the group were a couple of boys, including her beloved Derek Jones who she'd had a crush on for months. It was the very group she'd have been with if her mother had let her come out on her own.

She tried to keep her mother's tweed-clad bulk between herself and the gang, hoping they wouldn't see her, or recognise her in the suit. It could hardly be more different from her school uniform's sober shades of grey, or the jeans and T-shirts she wore from choice. Seen from behind she and her mother were just two middle-aged women out shopping together. If she turned her back and pretended to be someone else, someone old enough to wear the stupid suit, her friends would never know.

She'd forgotten about the reflective qualities of large plate-glass shop windows. Too late she looked up and saw the primrose mirror-image, stretched into an impossible caricature of herself. Too late she followed her own reflected gaze to where her friends were standing, and saw the dawning recognition in their equally distorted faces.

'Look, it's Jenny,' the mirror Gillian shrieked, and all the others turned bulbous heads and squat necks to stare. Jenny's mother, oblivious to the unfolding drama, began to tug her away, and Jenny felt caught between two equally unpleasant fates: a fly trapped between a shut window and a spider's web. Even as she turned to follow her mother she heard the screech as one of the unknown girls said, 'Oh God, look at her clothes! Look at the gloves!' Glancing back, the blood rushing upwards so she had a bright red face to clash with the yellow suit, she watched as eight pairs of eyes moved their gaze towards her hands. Eight mouths had dropped open, and eight different laughs broken out - and Derek Jones, damn him, had laughed the loudest of all.

At last! In the second-from-bottom drawer in the third chest she tried, her nail scraped against the plastic of the little pot of pills. She closed a hand round it and stood up, but even as she straightened a patch of dull yellow caught her eye - the finger of the rediscovered glove, trapped in the drawer above where she'd shut it in a rush.

'Jenny,' her mother called, in a breathless, fretful cry.

'Coming,' she replied, but oddly she didn't go straight to her mother's side. Instead she put the pills down on top of the chest and began re-opening the cupboards and drawers. She pulled out garments - a skirt here, a coat and scarf from somewhere else, and draped them over her arm. Only when she had a full set of clothes did she walk into her mother's room.

The old lady was propped against the pillows, covers drawn up to her chin and a blueish tinge around her lips. 'Hurry... you did find them?' she said, pausing for breath between every couple of words.

'Yes, yes,' said Jenny, piling the clothes on the bed. 'Don't worry about anything. I'll soon have you right as rain.' Pulling back the sheets she hauled her mother's nightgown over her head, revealing the pasty, wasted flesh. She took a blouse - a pretty, dainty thing - and began to push her mother's arms into the sleeves. The buttons no longer quite met across her mother's bust, but it didn't matter because it would be covered by the coat. When she'd arranged the blouse she turned her attention to the skirt. It was an old fashioned one with shirring and an elasticated waist, and slid on over her mother's spreading hips. After that it was the turn of the coat, and hat, and scarf, and shoes.

Her mother struggled weakly, the blue noticeably stronger now against the pallor of her face. 'Stop.... Jenny! What... are you doing?'

'Dressing you, of course,' Jenny said. 'We have to do things properly, don't we? Can't let people see you in this state where you're going. You have to dress nicely, you know. You have to keep your standards up.' As a last act she took the single yellow glove and drew it onto her mother's hand over the crinkled, blue-veined skin. 'There. That's better, isn't it? Now you're dressed really nicely.'

Still she made no move to fetch the pills. She'd get them in a minute, perhaps, but for now she simply stood back and watched. Her mother tried to speak but although her mouth opened and closed no words came out. But in the last few seconds her eyes fixed on Jenny's own, and she knew her mother understood.

Craig Douglas

Craig lives in Germany with his Belorussian wife and bilingual son who like nothing more than take the piss out of him in Russian. He is a Sergeant in the Army and looking forward to his last two years after which he plans to go on the 'rock and roll', living off his pension.

Perfect Symmetry

There's no shame in crying.

The moment Billy threw the spanner at Mr Radestock I knew the day would end in tragedy. The perfect image transcended through my many years, returning to me at night; its image spinning through the air in perfect symmetry toward its target. Back then we had a sofa, which had been an addition to our camp since the owner had thrown it out. The neighbour had puzzled at its disappearance just minutes after putting it out into the yard.

Billy bashed the crab against a wall and scraped meat out with a penknife. He passed me a portion of white meat. I could still taste the salt from the morning sea. He twisted a leg off and threw it at me with a flick of his hand, laughing. I caught it and crushed the carapace with my teeth and sucked the contents out. We both lay, not sure what to do with ourselves. The summer holidays would drag its heels nearer the end of August, bringing with it a boredom that would necessitate careless abandon and destruction.

'Fancy doin' that up?' Billy pointed a crab at a bike. It was a Chopper and looked in need of a make over.

'Ain't got no tools.'

'Got this.' He held up the spanner, which caught the sun - flashing silver in my eyes.

We pulled the Chopper from the bushes and inspected it. Its rear wheel had been bent beyond shape and the front one missing. The frame was still in good condition. All we needed was a pair of wheels.

'Howay,' Billy beckoned. He was off with a sprint and a skip to the gate. He grinned at me and I knew the look in his eyes would mean trouble.

'Mum'll be back soon.'

'Dinnae worry, man. We'll be back before she is. Howay.'

He began to whistle and swaggered off down the baking street.

When I sidled by him the flash of silver stabbed at my sight. I had to look again to see the adjustable spanner as it flipped in his hand. He flashed me a mischievous grin. 'Beetroot's got a load of stuff in his back yard. Must be a wheel in there some-where.'

'We'll get knacked if we're caught.'

The road ran with young blood, their shouts evoked a yearning for youth in the old. Rheumy eyes glimmered at the street in envy. Hands trembled as they brought tea to lips long silent. The chartered lands they'd crossed trailed a flower of memories; from halcyon moments to desperate, yet good times. They slurped tea and waited their turn to the grave. It was an inevitability that many chose to hide from, in their council estate tombs.

Young guns on bikes wheelied up and 'Evil Kneiveled' over ramps. Dogs ran amok, yap yapping, screwing, shitting and peeing. Mothers screamed and the world turned.

He gave me a look before clambering over the bricked wall to Mr Radestock's yard. Come on, it said. I knew the look so I followed into the deep grass. We turned over boxes of broken toys; spinning tops, burst balls, sodden comics and twisted bikes.

'Gis a hand..'

We yanked at a bike and ripped up grass. The door to the house thundered shut and the sky seemed to darken. My sight swam as I spun around to see this man at the open doorway. His eyes were stripped of all dignity and bared a wounded beast, open to the sky and to us.

'Freak!' Billy laughed and I remember the tool. It turned end over end until it reached the window, shattering it and the silence. The howl of anguish or the window's plea spurred both of us into flight.

This vein held my childhood memories in its very existence. I was wheeled up here one day and I swore I could see Billy grinning back at me at the gate. His dusty face accentuated the ivory teeth and his chicory eyes. His candy floss hair would catch the sun and hold it in its strands.

'Grandad's crying again,' my granddaughter gives a sigh, but she doesn't see Billy running from Mr Radestock. She doesn't see the car: or my brother, flying in perfect symmetry.

Patrick Belshaw

Some days Patrick can scarcely remember his own name, so it is sometimes good for him to be reminded that he has a PhD (Newcastle), is the author of 'A Kind of Private Magic', a group biography featuring E.M. Forster, and has had short stories published in several anthologies. Obviously the coolest of which is entitled '*Radgepacket*'.....obviously...!

Grey's Elegy

Russell Grey's wife died one day in late August.   He kept her body in the house for three weeks and two days. It would have been even longer, except he left the door open when he went outside to his little greenhouse in the back garden to pick some tomatoes for her lunch, and the Electric Man called.

He got quite a shock, the Electric Man, as he made his customary way through the sitting room to the little porch where the meters were housed.   The weather had been very warm - an Indian summer, folk said - and Rosemary Grey was propped up on the settee smothered in furs and a large double duvet.   The central heating was full on, and a large coal fire was burning in the grate.   Flies swarmed around the dead woman's head and around the remains of several plates of food left out on the low coffee table. Scores of them made a bee-line for the sweat on the Electric Man's face and hands as he dialled 999 on his mobile phone.

There was quite a scene when the police and the medics arrived.   Russell's mind had been knocked out of kilter. He couldn't understand why they wanted to take his wife away. 'Thirty-seven years,' he kept repeating, 'together thirty-seven years.   Please don't take her, she was just cold, poor dear.   So cold.' He shuddered, as if to emphasize the point. 'That's why I added the duvet.'

He stared vacantly into space. 'Just cold, that's all. Off her food, though, wouldn't touch a thing. Cooked all her favourites I did, but no, such a shame.   She hates waste, we both do, brought up during the war, you see.' He reached forward and clutched the doctor's arm. 'But she'll rally round, you'll see. Just needs more time. '

No one was listening.   Rosemary was taken away.   Then Russell was taken away. They were not taken away together. That was when Russell really lost it - when he was separated from Rosemary.   He fought like a cornered animal.   One of his flailing arms detonated a police constable's nose.   There was blood everywhere.

It was in all the papers, of course. On national television, even. The tiny village community was shocked - but not on reflection entirely surprised. The Greys were a devoted couple. They were never seen apart. They had always done everything together. Russell was never seen in the village again.

The Psychiatric Wing of the local hospital was called The Grove, perhaps because it backed onto a huddle of mature trees that had once been part of a wide expanse of mixed woodland belonging to the adjoining Lovett Estate. Occasionally, a patient would be seen walking among the trees in the grove. Not one of the paranoiacs, of course. Leaves whispering in the wind, as they sometimes did, could be very threatening to certain patients. But Russell, seeking solace, was soon a regular out there. The trees were his friends, he said. More dependable than people. People betrayed you. They took your loved ones from you. And they told lies. (Had they not told him that his wife was dead?) You could talk to trees. They didn't argue with you. They didn't try to persuade you to think the way they were thinking. They were neutral; they didn't judge. They listened patiently. They didn't mind you shouting at them, as he sometimes did - as you do from time to time, even with friends.

If not exactly popular - by nature, and by his condition, he kept himself to himself - Russell was a well-liked member of The Grove community. Mainly by the staff, it was true - but also by those of his fellow-patients who were able to form relationships. It was hardly surprising. He was polite, mild-mannered and even-tempered. There had been no repercussion of the violence he had demonstrated on the day he was forcibly taken away from his home. Delusional patients could present as quite normal individuals much of the time. As long as their delusions weren't challenged, they could rub along quite smoothly with those around them. In Russell's case, it helped (certainly, with the staff) that he was well-spoken and that his manners were refined. He had quickly acquired the reputation of being something of a gent. Somewhat predictably, he was soon known to staff and patients alike as The Earl.

He continued to protest that Rosemary was still alive, of course. But for the time being, this belief was allowed to go uncontested. To look at him, calmly going about his business, observing the routines of the place, you would never guess that he had a serious psychological problem - so much so that visitors and new patients usually mistook him for a member of staff. The closest he came to exhibiting behaviour that in any way might be regarded as bizarre - the word appeared to have some significance in the psychiatric community - occurred several weeks after his admission. By then Autumn was well under way, and Russell was observed walking among the trees, picking up leaves and bagging them, complaining as he laboured: 'They're so untidy! Love them all, of course. Love them to bits, every one of them. But I'm sick of picking up after them. Days getting shorter, too. And colder. Fine time to be taking your clothes off!'

The bags of leaves - at one point there were close on a dozen - began to clutter his room. The cleaners complained that there were so many littering the floor, some of them spilling their contents, that they couldn't do their job properly. The matter became so serious that the senior psychiatrist became involved. Russell was interviewed. Sensitively, of course. Well, he liked the colours, he said. And their different shapes. He liked the smell of them, too, and the crackly sound they made when you disturbed them. Could he keep just some of the bags, he pleaded. A long discussion ensued. Eventually, an offer was negotiated. One large bag of leaves - and no more. The senior psychiatrist, Dr Armstrong, was impressed with Russell's willingness to compromise. He recorded as much in his notes.

Autumn deepened. The trees in the grove had shed almost all of their gaudy, tattered clothing. Their forlorn trunks and limbs and branching fingers could be seen black and wet against the setting sun. It disturbed Russell to see them in this condition. Their arms seemed to be thrown up to the sky, as if pleading for some respite from the cold. But their entreaties went unheeded. Temperatures began to fall, and in an increasingly chilly wind the naked branches would sometimes shiver visibly. Some of the older trees would creak and groan, complaining among themselves about the cold getting into their joints. Russell shivered and suffered with them - for he refused to walk warmly-clad among his friends. They, poor things, had little or nothing to wear. How could he flaunt his advantage? The very thought was obscene.

One day in early December, Russell went missing for a few hours. He did not appear for lunch: that was when a search was instigated. The first place they looked was the grove, of course; but there was no sign of him in there. No sign of him anywhere, in fact. The search was extended to the main building, and finally to the grounds of the hospital. Then suddenly - at a point when the police were about to be involved - the hunt was called off. Russell had been found in his beloved grove after all. No one had thought to check it out again.

It was Adrian, one of the gardeners, who found him. Russell was perched three rungs from the top of a long metal ladder, which was propped up against the bough of an old oak tree. A large bag hung from a length of string slung around his waist. Every couple of minutes or so, he dipped a hand into this bag before reaching up into the branches of the tree. By now it was getting on for three o'clock, with the light beginning to fade. Adrian couldn't make out what Russell was doing. But whatever it was, it demanded all his attention. Rapt in his work, he seemed totally unaware that he was being observed.

'Ah, there you are!' Adrian had called up, grasping the foot of the ladder with two strong hands, vibrating it slightly. 'Glad I've found you. High and low, we've been searching. You old rogue! Led us a right dance, you have.' Russell had ignored him. Absorbed in his task, he had carried on. Adrian caught a movement in one of the branches. 'Best come down, eh? Dark soon. Could get tricky then. What're you doing up there, any road?'

'What does it look like?'

'Don't know. Can't see in this light. What's in the bag?'

'Leaves, of course.' Russell had lowered his hands, and had turned his body to look down. 'One of the gardeners, aren't you - yes?   Well, you of all people should know about my friends in here. Winter's coming on. You must have noticed? Poor things, they're going to freeze unless we get some clothes back on them. Believe me, I know. Take my word, I know about these things. So that's what I'm - oh, bugger! Now look what's happened. I've got glue on my hands.'

'Not sure I've quite got your drift, my friend,' Adrian had called up. 'But whatever you're doing, best get down now, eh? You can't work in the dark.'

'Don't want to come down,' Russell had cried. 'Job unfinished.' His voice was cracking. Was he crying, Adrian had wondered?   'But anyway - I can't come down. Not now. I seem to be stuck to the ladder!'

Someone had to come from the hospital.   He came with a ladder, a patient manner and a special solvent. He left unable to conceal a smile. Russell was left to face a new round of friendly chats with Dr Armstrong. Dr Armstrong also wore a smile. Such a nice man, Russell thought. Everyone was very kind and friendly. But only Dr Armstrong seemed to understand why the sticking-back-on of the leaves had been so important to him.

Winter set in.   Snow. Rain. Cloud. Wind. Occasional sunshine - but usually accompanied by numbing cold.   The sort of weather that didn't encourage walks among the trees. Not that Russell was able to go out for several weeks. He went down with pneumonia, and his convalescence was slow. He found it difficult to regain his former vigour. More worryingly, he seemed to have lost all interest in life. He fretted about the fate of his beloved trees. He shut himself away whenever possible. He seemed to hibernate within himself. He began to exhibit signs of depression. Dr Armstrong and his team were worried.

Caroline, Russell's daughter, was summoned from New Zealand.   She left behind her rosy-cheeked apple-grower, Reuben, and her two teenage girls.   But not for long, she hoped. God willing, this business with her Dad would soon be settled one way or another. These things took time, she realized. People grieved in different ways. But for heaven's sake, it had been months now! Maybe the last throw of the dice, the doctor had said. So, yes - she was willing to give it another go. 'But don't hold your breath,' she had warned. They had never been close, she and her Dad. His cosy intimacy with her mother had always left her feeling excluded.

She was given a room in the Wing. To be near her father. So they could talk. There was a lot of talking - on her part, anyway. She observed a change in him. A change for the better, perhaps? He seemed less prickly, much more resigned.

With Dr Armstrong's blessing, she decided to take him to the place where her Mother's ashes were scattered. The site was a limestone outcrop on the southern slopes of Wild Boar Hill, a peaceful spot overlooking a ribbon of water that wound its ways through the narrow valley below. It was less than a mile from the road, and no more than a hundred yards or so to the east of the main footpath. Yet it felt remote. She hired a taxi for the twelve-mile round trip. It waited for them in the small lay-by tucked into the foot of the hill.

'Why have we come here?' Russell asked.

'I told you, remember?' Caroline took a cushion from her bag for him to sit on. 'To be near Mum.'

'No,' Russell said. His voice was low, but firm. 'Your Mother's in the hospital. Be out soon. I told you - remember? So why are we here?'

'Okay, Dad, have it your way.' Caroline was counting to ten.

'Let's say we're here so that I can be close to Mum.'

'Sorry...?'

'She loved this spot, Dad. Don't you remember?'

'No, I don't. Never been here before.'

'Yes, you have. Dozens of times. Honestly, Dad - your favourite view.' She turned to look at him and attempted a smile. Her shock tactics were not working. She looked at the view again. 'Well, anyway - I feel close. Let's leave it at that, shall we?'

Hearing the crack in her voice, she paused.   'She's only three feet away.   So, yes - I feel close.'   She turned her head again.   'Bit of a shock for me as well, you know - living on the other side of the world.'

Russell didn't respond.   He stared at the ground ahead of them.   For several quiet, painful minutes, he simply sat, still as the rock beneath him, and stared at the ribs of limestone poking through the short, sheep-nibbled grass.

'God, it's cold here.' he said suddenly, and he shuddered. 'And the ground - so bare!   What a dreadful place to be.   I want to go, please.   I want to leave.   Please will you take me away?'

A fortnight after Caroline went back to North Island, New Zealand, Russell went missing again.   This time, the police were involved.   This time, Dr Armstrong and his team were seriously concerned.   The search went on for thirty-six hours, and there was still no sign of him.   Eventually - in retrospect, perhaps it should have been done sooner? - Caroline was contacted again.   She told them about the visit to Wild Boar Hill. She gave them the name of the taxi firm she had used - and yes, a man fitting Russell's description had hired a cab the previous day.   It was a one-way fare.

The search party arrived at the outcrop towards late afternoon on the second day.   In front of the memorial seat they found a pile of men's clothing, neatly folded, covering the ground like a blanket. Socks, rolled neatly into a pair of shoes, were found alongside.   A large piece of limestone had been placed on top of the clothing, presumably to stop it blowing away in what was known locally as a 'thin' wind.   There was no sign of Russell.

He was found twenty minutes later in a right-angled corner between two dry stone walls, about a quarter of a mile up the slope.   It was a place obviously favoured by sheep seeking refuge from the elements.   There was a strong smell of droppings, and scraps of wool caught in the crevices between the stones were being spun in small spirals of air that had breached the sheltering wall.

Russell was stark naked and curled up like a foetus.   His

neat, close-together knees were drawn up to his chest, and his arms were bent across his body, as if for warmth. He was, however, as cold as the stone around him. And his lifeless body was so stiff that his knee-joints had later to be broken before he could be laid out.

Ray Banks

Ray is the author of five books, four of which feature his private eye Callum Innes, as well as a clutch of short stories and a novella. He lives in Newcastle-upon-Tyne, and every now and then actually gets round to updating his website - *www.thesaturdayboy.com* - where he accepts both visitors and gifts of hard liquor.

The Deacon Shuffle

'What you gonna do, Joey?'

Dunc brings it up the day the two of them get chucked out the hostel because Dunc had tack on him. And Dunc's already pure fucked off because the way he sees it, it's medicinal and it's only tack, man. It's only fuckin' resin. When he doesn't get an answer, he looks down at the bin bag full of clothes by his feet. Sticks a rollie in his mouth. He takes up a double seat on the Metro, his legs spread, his spine curved. There's the sound of plastic every time he moves his foot.

Still nothing from his mate across the way, so Dunc starts on: 'Where you gonna go, Joey? Tony Hills, man, he's dead or fucked off somewhere. Your old lads Andy and Blake up in Blyth, they got themselves nicked. So what you got left, man? You want to nip down The Well, see Goose? Gonna put up with all that Falklands shite to get a fuckin' score bag?'

Dunc smokes half his rollie in one draw. Smoke puffs out of his mouth as he continues.

'Fuckin' Tumbledown, man,' says Dunc. 'That cunt bashed Argies like I bashed his fuckin' mam.'

Joey's breathing through his mouth. 'Don't matter. I can't go back in there, can I?'

Joey isn't his birth name, but it's what everyone calls him. Name stuck to him like grem. Dunc used to call him a streak of dehydrated piss, so that's mates for you. Dunc always gets a vocabulary - 'a certain perspicacity' - once he's tied off on one.

Now Joey's got his cap pulled down, two days of blond fuzz on his cheeks and neck. Sitting forward, leaning on his knees, head down. Smoke curls from the inside of his palm, his tab turned inwards just in case the inspectors come round. Looks like his hand's on fire. And it fits in with the full-on boiling temperature on the train. Dunc doesn't give a shit about the heat or his tab. He's got his shirt off, the blue ink on his back like a dare, the tracks on his arms double-dogging it.

Dunc says, 'You want revenge or not?'

'Revenge?' Joey catches a face of smoke and blinks before he turns his face to the window. 'Howeh, man, it's not that fuckin' bad.'

'You know your problem, Joey? You're a fuckin' mong, can't see straight. Tapped, man. Always have been.'

'She'll recognise us.'

'So what if she does?'

'So she knows me name, she knows where I live.'

'Like I fuckin' care.' Dunc spreads his legs further, gets more comfortable. 'Like you fuckin' care, man. You don't live there no more anyway.'

'I don't want the polis coming round me mam's.'

Dunc sucks his teeth, shakes his head. 'I dunno, like. If it was me, I'd want a bit of fuckin' payback. You been moaning on for ages, like that bitch was on your back every time you went in. Treat you like a smackhead thief an' that, you want to do something about it.'

'Can't do nowt about it, Dunc. I'm barred, like.'

''Cause of what? 'Cause you twocked a couple fuckin' Mars Bars?'

Joey poked at something in his back tooth with his tongue. It was only a couple of Mars Bars - Work, Rest and Nick - but that suspicious old bitch, she'd kept Action Man eagle eyes on him the whole time. Thinking back, Joey should've known better, learned from his mistakes. But the urge to steal was too strong and he had a sweet tooth. When he turned around, she'd been straight up, caught him with a fistful of kets. Shouldn't have been a big deal problem, but Joey'd been nabbed before and this was his third strike.

She went off it, pure mental - looked to Joey like her eyes would roll back in their sockets, she'd point and scream like one of them pod people he'd seen on the telly. Joey did the Deacon Shuffle, one foot to the other, acted like he didn't know what was happening, tried to block out this woman's kick-off.

'Kinda situation's that?' says Dunc. 'What you gonna do then, eh? You admit you nicked stuff, you're out. You don't admit it, she's still got your fuckin' script.'

'I know.'

'And you went down the market, right?'

'Aye.'

'Aye. With the fuckin' Motorolas. You need cash so bad, you risk getting nicked down the market over phones?' Dunc leans forward, slaps Joey's cap. 'Give it a shake, marra.'

Joey frowns and adjusts the peak. Pulls it even lower to hide the red in his face. 'Didn't know what I was thinking, like.'

'Fuckin' bitch. Reckons she can hold your jellies over you like they're fuckin' dog treats. All that power's gone to her head. And while I'm fuckin' at it, what kind of power is it, anyway? Give 'em a white coat, they think they're a doctor.' Dunc finishes his tab, drops and grinds what's left of the Zig-Zag into the rubber floor of the train. 'All I'm saying, we do this, we don't need to score for fuckin' donkeys'.'

Joey doesn't say anything. He looks at the trampled rollie, takes a drag on his own.

'You'll do this,' says Dunc.

Nothing from Joey.

The doors hiss open at Manors.

****

Dunc doesn't let it go. Joey knows he won't, but he still bristles when Dunc swans into his room at the Sally. Joey shifts in bed, still half-asleep, and the room goes black for an instant, something landing on his face.

He hears Dunc saying, 'No excuses now.'

Joey puts one hand up to his head, pulls the ski mask from his face. 'Aw, howeh…'

'No excuses. Stick that on your head, that old woman won't know you from her fuckin' son. Camera won't get you, neither. So any shite you come up with now, it's 'cause you're a bottling cunt.'

Joey rubs the material of the ski mask. The heat'll kill him if he wears this. He pauses and bites a hangnail from his thumb, then sticks his fingers through the eyeholes.

There's a weight on the bed. Joey looks up. The door to his room is closed, Dunc leaning against the wall with a grin on his face. Joey follows his gaze. A machete lies on the bed. Rusty at the blade, crusty at the handle.

'What's that?' says Joey.

'That, marra, is a big fuck-off knife. Stick that under your jacket, we're in business.'

Joey's already shaking his head. 'Where'd you get it from?'

'Fuck does it matter?'

Joey puts his hand on the machete, lifts it. He feels the weight, the balance, in his hand and arm. The crust along the handle is a mucky brown.

'I can't carry this,' he says.

'Course you can.'

'Dunc -'

'Unless you're a bottler.'

'I'm not -'

'You keep this shit up, you're a bottling cunt. End of.'

Silence.

Joey thinks about the machete, about what Dunc wants to do. His lips go thin. He blinks.

'What you got?' says Joey.

Dunc opens his jacket, grabs the rubber handle sticking from his inside pocket. He draws out a claw hammer. Looks new.

'See anyone fucking about with us, I'll put a hole in their napper.' He short-swings the hammer. 'Wap. Down. Out.'

Joey pictures that hammer coming down on someone's skull. He blinks some more. 'This is shite, man.'

Dunc replaces the hammer, the grin dropping to half his face. There's a glitter in his eyes. He opens the door.

'The morra, Joey,' he says. 'First thing. We're on.'

When Dunc closes the door behind him, Joey gets a burning pain in his throat.

****

Joey has plenty of time to think that night. He needs it. He's been bombarded by Dunc all day. Spent the afternoon with him, but they didn't talk about the next morning in detail. Dunc dropped statements into the conversational lulls, and now Joey's trying to piece them together, his stare trained on the ceiling.

Dunc said, 'You been in there before, Joey. You know the place like your own cock.'

Dunc said, 'You think the fuckin' polis care about a chemist? They got people stabbing each other and raping each other every day. They're not gonna be bothered about a shitty little methadone rip.'

Dunc said, 'Them fuckers, that bitch what fucked you over, they're all the same. You want to worry about them you be my fuckin' guest, but I'll tell you this: it don't matter who's in there. People at them cushy jobs, they think that if they fuck with people they see every day - people like you and me, man - they're like better than those people, know what I mean?'

Joey knows. He's sick of it. He went in there to get his methadone, reckoned he was turning his life around. Back on the straight and narrow. That bitch behind the counter giving him evils, it wasn't good for a man's soul, especially when it was as fractured as Joey's.

And then there's that fuckin' name. Not his name. His name's Robert, named after his dad, wherever the fuck he is. Only his mam who calls him Robert.

To everyone else, he's Joey.

Back in the eighties, back when Robert was a kid, Blue Peter's annual charity thing - collect your milk bottle tops, all that - was for the disabled. In order to do that, in order to really grab the kids' attention, the BBC brought on Joey fuckin' Deacon. Poor bastard had cerebral palsy, proper shoulder-biter, looked like Davros in a charity shop suit. And kids, being the spiteful little cunts they were, they adopted Joey Deacon as their spastic poster boy. His name became a byword for any freak - physical, mental, even spiritual. Something the matter with you, you didn't fit the norm, you didn't belong, you acted like a divvy that one time or accidentally called the teacher 'Mam', you were a Joey. That was it, you were branded. Kids saw you, their tongues got stuck under their bottom lip, the Frances McDormand thing. Their heads went to one shoulder - maybe there'd be a slap to the back of one wrist - and the word 'Deeeaaacon' came at you like a punch to the gut. Or Flid, Scoper, Bifta...

And this particular Joey, he lapses every now and then. Like when he's got Dunc staring at him, the smoke spilling from the big man's mouth, sucked up his nose and recycled. That glitter in Dunc's eyes, it makes him feel like a Joey because he's so frightened.

He puts a hand over his face. Pinches his nose and screws his eyes closed. Joey feels like he's about to cry, but he doesn't allow himself that luxury anymore. His body shakes under the sheet. He waits it out, his face creased. Hears the bedsprings squeak as he shudders.

The emotion passes. Joey lets go of his nose, sniffs a wet breath to his lungs.

Breathes out and wipes his cheeks.

He pulls himself out of bed, reaches under the mattress and removes the machete. Joey turns the weapon in his hand, puts one finger to the blade and draws it down. The blade's dull.

Joey's scared. But he's always been scared.

****

Dunc goes into the chemist first. He's safe to show his face - he's never been in there before and the woman behind the counter isn't going to recognise him. It's early morning and the heat hasn't settled into the day yet, but Joey's still sweating. He can feel himself burning up inside, one hand on the machete inside his jacket, the other dug deep into his pocket, rubbing the ski mask like a security blanket. He stands across the street from the chemist, trying to look like he's meant to be there.

So Dunc's inside, he's doing a recce. Making sure the place is clean of customers, making sure there's nobody caught in a blind spot, nobody who'll get in the way when all this kicks off. He has a look through the greetings cards on the spinning rack, then goes to the door.

Joey sees Dunc appear, sees him nod. Joey pulls the ski mask over his head with one hand, pulls the eyeholes to the right position. Then he jogs across the road, picking up speed as he hits the threshold and into the chemist.

The more noise, the better. Get the woman scared out of her mind, she won't remember a fuckin' thing. Someone comes on all aggressive, a person gets scared, the brain shuts down. Joey knows all about that - he's been there enough times. Could be Satan himself telling her to empty the fuckin' till, she won't know the difference. So when Joey bursts into the chemist, he's waving the machete like a cavalry sword and screaming.

It's like Dunc says: these people, they never expect it to happen to them.

Dunc slams himself up against the till, gestures for Joey to follow. Joey holds the machete high as he squeezes behind the counter, takes the two steps in a single jump. The woman scrabbles out of the way, backs into a corner. She's silent, but her mouth is open like a scream is caught in her throat. It's not the old bitch, either. This woman's young. Got a Celtic band tattooed on her wedding finger. Her eyes shine with tears, but the water doesn't escape. Joey points the machete at her, uses every muscle in his arm to stop the tip from shaking. She flinches, stares at the blade.

Joey can hear Dunc in the back. He's pulling drawers out, the rustle of the bin bag as he empties the pills and potions into it.

Joey wonders why the old bitch isn't here. He wants to ask this girl, but he can't speak. And anyway, it's like, think, you spacka: he asks about the old bitch, they're going to know who he is. They're going to go looking for him at his mam's house. And Joey's mam always believed Joey had something special in him.

He doesn't want to think about that now.

Joey looks at the girl. She's got a badge on her uniform that reads CAMRYN. Joey narrows his eyes behind the mask, wonders what kind of name that is. Starts to play on him, that name. What kind of parent calls their kid Camryn? And now he stares at the ring finger, part of the hand that's covering her face. He wonders why she got that tattoo, wonders who it's for.

Too many questions.

Before he knows it, Dunc's back out and slapping him on the shoulder.

'Howeh, Joey,' he says. 'We're gone, marra.'

Joey doesn't move for a moment. Then he shuffles his feet, not sure what to do. He hears Dunc knock the card rack over on his way out the door. He looks down at the girl. There's a puddle of urine on the floor.

'Sorry,' he says.

And runs.

****

Dunc lies back on the grass, the handle of the claw hammer lolling out of his inside pocket. He's taken two vallies and he's drifting. The sun beats down on him. There's a Morrisons' carrier full of beer on the ground. Joey reaches for another can, cracks it. Out the back of the flats now, nobody's going to bother them, so Joey's got the machete laid out on the grass in front of him. He looks at it as he drinks. He's taken a couple of blue pills himself, didn't know what they were but they're doing a similar job to Dunc's.

Joey pictures Camryn's face, blank with fear. He pictures the piss on the floor, the Celtic ring. He pictures all of these things swirling around like water down a plughole. His gut feels weird, so he drinks some more beer. It doesn't help. It makes him want to throw up. Joey looks across at Dunc. The big man grins at him.

'Did alright in there, Joey,' he says.

Joey scratches his bottom lip with his top teeth, looks at his can.

'Should be good for a couple weeks until the next one.'

'Nah,' says Joey.

Dunc lets out a hack of a laugh. It sounds ugly. 'Said that the last time, Joey.'

'I know. And I mean it this time.'

'Aye, right y'are.'

Joey stares at him. 'I fuckin' mean it.'

'I know.' Dunc sits up, puts a hand to his head. Then he pulls his T-shirt off to top up his homegrown tan. 'But you do what I tell you to fuckin' do else I'll deck you.'

Joey nods, sniffs.

Dunc lies back on the grass and closes his eyes. There's a sick grin on his face. It makes his lips look purple and wet.

Joey puts his can on the grass and reaches for the machete.

'Aye,' says Joey. 'I know you will.'

****

Joey's upstairs, lying on his bed, looking at the Loaded poster he's got on the ceiling. Jennifer Ellison tries to look demure, stares back at him with her arse in the air.

Joey's mam opened the door to him and a look of terror spread across her face.

She was lucky Joey wasn't carrying the machete at the time. It might've killed her. But no, Joey had left it somewhere else. He wishes he hadn't. He liked the machete. It was like a sword and he always liked swords, especially when he was a kid. Like when he was playing by himself out in the back yard and he had this broom handle he was waving about. Fought off a bunch of soldiers like fuckin' Zorro. Jumped backwards onto the bin and missed his footing, ended up getting stitches in his head.

Only person he ever told about that was Dunc.

And Dunc said, 'That explains a lot.'

Joey sits up, looks at his front. His jacket, his T-shirt, his jeans. Blood caked brown on his clothes. He wishes he had the machete with him right now so he could compare the colours.

Joey picks at some of the dried blood on his jeans. He examines the flecks under his fingernail, then wipes his hand.

Dunc was right on a couple of things.

One: People freeze when the screaming starts.

Two: People never expect it to happen to them.

Joey remembers picking up the machete like he was going to offer it to Dunc, the blade lying across the palms of his hands like he'd seen in a samurai film. He knocked the beer over with his foot as he stood up.

Dunc opened his eyes, saw Joey with the machete, then looked down at the spilled beer. 'You fuckin' spaz.'

Then Joey started screaming. He twisted the machete, closed his fingers around the handle, brought the other hand round and the blade down on Dunc's leg. The machete dug deep and stuck. Dunc folded in two, his stomach muscles twitching as he sat up, the colour rushing from his face.

Joey frowned, tried to wriggle the blade free from Dunc's thigh. All he could hear was an ear-splitting screech. And he wondered where it was coming from. He let go of the machete, took a step back. Saw Dunc flailing about on the grass, blood welling around the blade, raining down the sides of his leg.

He stopped, watched Dunc some more.

Heard, 'You-fuckin'-cunt-you-fuck-gonna-fuckin'-kill-you.'

Then Joey ran.

After a while, Joey felt his knees ache with each step. He slowed down, looked over his shoulder. Knew that Dunc wouldn't be following, but he had to make sure. He got an image of his mam in his mind, telling him to stand up to bullies, all them lads at school who called him flid. He felt his chest tighten, had to stop. Put a hand over his face again. Let the heaves go through him.

Nothing left in him now. He's off the bed, at the window. There was a buzz at the door a second ago. Joey looks out the window at the police car.

He's glad. If it's the police, it's not Dunc. Dunc's off somewhere, bleeding to death. Or he's fixed up and ready to even the score.

Doesn't matter now.

Joey knew his mam wouldn't let this go. She probably thinks he's mixed up in something serious. She's probably right. Because Joey thinks this wouldn't have happened if he hadn't been such a fuckin' Scoper. A fuckin' spaz. A fuckin' Deacon.

He feels a cold sweat at the sound of someone climbing the stairs.

There's a knock, then the door opens.

Joey turns.

Two uniforms on the landing, looking serious and disgusted at the same time. One of them talking to him, his lips barely moving. Saying something, but Joey turns back to the window, blocks the copper out. His feet are burning. He starts to shift the weight from one foot to the other.

And somewhere in the drone of the copper talking, he thinks he hears the name Robert, but he doesn't answer to it.

Darren Sant

Darren was first published in the poetry collection *'Before the Last Shadow Fades.'* He continues to inflict his writing on the world - despite the odd looks his wife gives him - and lives the troubled life of a Midlander in the great city of Hull, where they talk funny.

The Ungrateful Dead

The squeal of a badly played electric guitar assaulted my ears and for the third time that evening I wondered why the hell I did this job. Frenzied teens leapt around the mosh pit like rabid squirrels. My temples pounded in time to the drumbeat and I took a sip of JD and Coke to try and further deaden my senses.

Why the fuck had my editor given me this assignment? I'd never had a good word to say about this fucking band. I hated grunge. Looking around "The Temple" I wondered if I'd been in a grottier club. On reflection, yes, plenty. I knocked back the remainder of my drink weaved my way a little drunkenly to the toilet.

After a quick slash I admired the impressive pool of vomit in each and every fucking sink and stood at the back to watch The Ungrateful Dead's last few tracks. Shite name for a band anyway. Four members all pimply, overly pale, ugly, just about post teen, geeky, fuckwits to a man. There had been a lot of hype about them, they were on the rise and other hacks would have given their left bollock for the chance to do this interview.

There was talk that they regularly performed satanic rituals. The obligatory wild tales of groupie orgies and substance abuse. I'd heard it all before and it was no more believable now, but hey it filled venues and sold albums. Every whining, wanking spotty little tosspot wanted to be like them. Me? I was old school, too old to be writing for the mag I was writing for and regularly took out my spite on shitty little bands and in particular The Ungrateful Dead. It was a little bemusing my editor had insisted I do this. The twat never liked me anyhow. It promised to be a memorable interview.

The last chord echoed in my ears and I took ten minutes to have another JD before heading back stage. A bulldog with a sense of humour failure stood blocking the door to backstage. I showed him my pass and without a word he let me through. There were the usual hangers on in the corridor. Teenage girls, jail bait, wearing little in the way of clothing and prepared to

44

sacrifice their virginity and their dignity to be closer to their heroes. Lads stoned out of their heads, as interested in the girls in the corridor as the band. I rapped on the door and announced myself. A pale looking PR opened the door and ushered me in.

The room was, surprisingly dimly lit. There was trash all over the floor, empty bottles, pizza cartons; it looked like a teenager's bedroom only on a larger scale. The band idled in the corner passing each other a bottle of vodka and gulping deep. High from their set. The lead singer, Mickey, had his trousers round his ankles and an eager groupie was sucking on his cock as if it contained the elixir of life. I doubted it. But watching her little tight leather clad ass and her head bobbing up and down was kind of hypnotic.

I made like Bob the Builder and prepared to build some bridges.

'Great gig, guys. Fuckin' awesome.'

They smirked a little as they regarded me. The bass player, who the press called Scarecrow, on account of his penchant for old clothes and lack of personal hygiene, held up a back copy of our magazine and started to read.

'Sounding ten years out of date and looking about as attractive as an eighty year old nun with syphilis and a flesh eating disease The Ungrateful Dead will have a career as short as your average mayfly. Let's hope they'll soon be serving fries in fucking Burger King where they belong.'

I held up my hands in mock surrender.

'C'mon guys don't hold that against me. You know how the game is played. I knock you a little and we get three hundred letters of complaint and some turds in the post but we sell more issues.'

Scarecrow chose a few choice pieces from another couple of issues he had open ready on the desk. I was about ready to say fuck this and walk out when I heard a noise behind me. I looked over my shoulder as the bulldog stepped into the room.

He locked the door behind him.

'Hey what is this......'

Time stood still. Even the groupie had stopped her sucking and was regarding me whilst licking her lips. Her green eyes glinted in a way that looked chilling. I was sobering up fast. I was in for a kicking here and no messing. A furtive glance around the room showed there was no help from any quarter. Just the band, the bulldog, the PR, the cock loving groupie and me. I looked to Mickey, the front man, I nearly shat myself. His piercing denim blue eyes showed no mercy, but what unsettled me were his fucking TEETH. Pointed like a vampire's. He stared me straight in the eye as he grasped the groupies blond hair and pulled her up. She gave a delighted little squeal as she turned to face him. He leaned forward and sank his teeth into her throat. Blood spurted and he made suckling noises. I watched in horrified fascination as the blood ran from her neck to dribble in pools on the floor.

Fuck this I thought, recovering from frightened rabbit syndrome. I turned and barged the unsuspecting bulldog, ramming him in the gut. A swift knee to the knackers and he dropped like a stone. I clamoured at the door turning the key the muppet had left in it. I was away down the corridor and out the building panting in seconds. Wild eyed and suddenly sober I legged it down the street gibbering in fear.

* * * * *

Back in the club the band looked at one another. Mickey removed his fake teeth and the blond removed her blood pack. They all cracked up laughing.

Gareth J Mews

Gareth's finger is blatantly not on the pulse of society. He hates everything popular on principle with the exception of binge drinking and bacon sandwiches. He also has a particular penchant for lap dancing and cups of tea. He's an aggressive pacifist who will walk through walls for the people he is fond of and put through walls those who try to hurt them.

Where's Your Head At?

Do you ever get the feeling that you're being watched?

I get it all the time, not that I can know for sure of course. Whenever I'm walking down the street, sitting at the bus stop, even queuing in the newsagent, I get that unnerving notion of staring eyes trained on the back of my neck. My doctor tells me I'm paranoid, the few friends I have tell me I'm imagining things (although I can't imagine how I can imagine anything at all) and my therapist, smug twat that he is, tells me to stare back.

But you know the type? Every time you catch their eye, they look away, trying to make it look like they're just scanning the train, or the room, or the passing landscape. But they averted their eyes too sharply when you saw them. Embarrassed by their own curiosity. In their mind they'll convince themselves that they accept diversity 'The world is full of different people' they tell their friends 'Humans like you and me'. But when confronted with a breach in the status quo they stare, eyes wide, mouths open, their natural reactions betraying their ignorance. Never xenophobic at home, never racist among whites, tolerant in their own living room.

You see it's difficult for a man in my situation. Yes I have a disability and yes I am grateful that I still have the use of my arms and legs. With my affliction I find it hard to integrate with society, I never get invited to dinner parties or for drinks after work and while they may seem like trivial things to you, it all amounts to making it harder to come to terms with what I have (or haven't).

They say it's a mutation of alopecia. That's all they say. I first noticed it in my mid twenties when I lost all my body hair in the space of a year. At the time I wasn't bothered, I never need shave again, I had a skinhead anyway but the real bonus was that I'd never get crabs. The downsides of having no eyebrows and a pubic region like that of an eleven year old boy, were dismissed as minor inconveniences, after all there is a growing trend of men (and women) out there who prefer it that way.

The shock came a couple of years later.

My doctor had always told me that my form of the disease was not just straightforward hair loss. He said something about the chemicals used to sterilise water, a healthy diet of amphetamine, fags and beer, plus no-one yet fully understands the affects of mobile phones.

Disease?! What fucking disease, so I had no hair, I was in good shape, otherwise fit and healthy, beautiful girlfriend, enjoyable, varied job, opportunities for travel, what more could I want? So against his wishes I stopped seeing my doctor and settled back for a life as a happy, content, bald man.

Then one morning my head fell off.

You know when you're a kid and your second teeth are coming through? Some of them wobble for weeks, you push them, pull them, twist and tweak them and they hang in there forever; and some just drop into the sink when you're brushing your teeth? That's what happened with my head.

It's an unnerving feeling, watching your confused body stumble around the bathroom, stabbing at thin air with a frothy tooth brush. I couldn't call for help; the shock had rendered me speechless. Even if it hadn't, every time I opened my mouth the running tap filled it with water. After about twenty minutes I'd managed to roll my head out of the wet sink and onto the floor, by which time my decapitated body had fallen into the bath and knocked itself unconscious.

It was time to take stock of the situation.

Fact 1: My head had just fallen into the sink; a bad thing.

Fact 2: Against the rules of modern medicine, I was not dead; a good thing (perhaps).

Fact 3: My body, which until now, I had found useful to get myself around was motionless in the bath; a bad thing.

Fact 4: My girlfriend wanted to be in the bathroom; definitely a bad thing.

Shit, think fast. Think, that's about all I could do from now on. This was the precursor to the rest of my life. If I couldn't think on my feet (poor turn of phrase) then what could I do?

The poor girl took it quite badly. When you think about it it's hard not to over react when you burst through your bathroom door to see the love of your life lying face down in the bath. Only he's not face down, his dismembered head is dripping at your feet asking for a towel.

I still see her sometimes, although often she refuses my visits. She says she just can't look me in the face anymore. I don't blame her; I probably would have done the same thing. Although I would like to think that I could be trusted with sharp objects and that I didn't still get hysterical at the sight of a football.

The next year was a blur. I became a lab rat for the mavericks, humanitarians and hot shots of the medical world. The government kept me out the papers and kept me underground. I was prodded, probed, scanned and tested for hours on end. Still they couldn't find an answer. According to their results I was a healthy headless man. I would never suffer from acne or hay fever and head colds were a thing of the past. My liver had seen better days but then, whose hasn't? I spent my time reflecting on what I could never do again; kiss, lick, suck. I thought about sex a lot but I always thought about sex, that's what kept me going, that's what got me down.

They let me keep my head. The lack of blood supply had made it whither but I couldn't smell it so I didn't mind. I used to find it comforting to hug it like a teddy as I went to sleep. The doctors said they found it unnerving but it was my head and I'd got quite attached to it over the years.

Eventually I had to let them take it. The teeth were falling out and I kept losing the bottom jaw. We gave it a proper burial. I had always been of a slightly morbid disposition and had bought a burial plot in my hometown. The ceremony was conducted under the cover of darkness, at least I assume it was dark, it was the only time I was ever allowed out. I lowered my skull in its small square coffin six feet deep to await the rest of me, set to arrive in matching attire some time soon.

For days I couldn't sleep. I tossed and turned all night and was restless and irritable all day. I tried sleeping in the bed, on the floor, on my front, side and back without joy and usually I was asleep as soon as my head hit the pillow. They made me a new head. A papier-mâché one at first but I kept rolling on it and scratching myself on the wire inside. I kept telling them that it would have my eye out one day and all the bastards did was laugh.

One day they brought me my new head, made by the props department at some movie studio. It was my head, I don't mean 'Finally a head that belongs to me' but my fucking head. They had sent old photos and measurements and what came back was an exact replica of what my head looked like that fateful day, minus the chicken pox scar above the left eye. They had added hair but I asked for it to be removed. I was never particularly fond of it when I had it and besides, I always liked to stand out in a crowd.

There are many disadvantages to not having a head. Although, bizarrely, I could still hear and talk. The engineers had devised a complex tracheotomy, which allowed me to speak, after a fashion. It wasn't my normal voice; I sounded more like a gremlin that smokes sixty a day. Anyone who has subjected themselves to the wonders of heavy, prolonged smoking will know how difficult it is to stop. I have always conformed to the view that I have the right to contract lung cancer if I so wish. It is a basic human right to destroy the body you're in before it destroys you. So there was no way that I was going to allow a trivial matter of having no mouth and only the remnants of a throat to make me quit. It was one of the few comforts I had left, why not become a statistic? One in three people will contract cancer but no-one until now could live without their head. It was difficult at first but with perseverance I came through. In the early days when I only had a stump, I could inhale through my exposed trachea. The only problems were that I couldn't grip the fag and I kept flicking ash down my gullet. By the time my new head had arrived the engineers had grafted a sphincter to the top of my windpipe and reinforced my epiglottis. So now I can smoke through the top of my stump with my fire retardant head attached.

Have you ever seen a man swallow a lit cigarette and walk along merrily with smoke billowing out of his ears?

No?

Me neither but apparently it's one hell of a sight.

I got thrown out on the streets after a year. Apparently when you are on a government contract they have to take you on permanently after twelve months or let you go. They turned me loose. Tax payers money was tight and what with government bank bailouts left right and centre, headless research had been put on the backburner. I found a bed-sit not far from the middle of town. High crime, low rent. Smackheads, pit bulls and tracksuit bottoms. My ground floor room got broken into on the first night, there was nothing to steal and when they were presented with my head on the bed-side table and my stump snoring on the pillow, they didn't hang around. That was the only trouble I got. I'd walk down the street, crunching through the broken glass and dog shit and people left me alone. Only that feeling of being watched.

What amazed me was the job opportunities open for a man who couldn't see what was right in front of his face. Within a week of leaving the research centre I started work at the job centre. Sitting, staring blankly ahead with no expression on your face is apparently a highly desirably trait. I was guaranteed an interview under their disabled policy and I was sure that someone would suspect that I had no obvious physical disability but then I realised that they saw able bodied folk everyday that were pretending to be crocked and they never noticed a thing. I didn't have many friends at work though. The only time to socialise was on a cigarette break and I couldn't smoke with the others. I had to walk round the corner, light up a fag and swallow it.

It was my lack of social interaction that got me down, not having people around to talk to can make even the most crowded city a very lonely place.

I often toyed with the idea of ending it all, topping myself. Even then my options were limited. The two most popular were way out of the question, I couldn't hang myself or blow my brains out. The sphincter on my throat prevented drowning and while I may be able to jump out of a window, I can never be sure that I'm not on the ground floor. So I decided to try night classes. Pilates was no good, I just got hit on by menopausal women who were over the moon to see a young man attending yoga for grannies. Kickboxing lasted three weeks until we started sparring. Asian cookery was fun until the heat from my steamer loosened the seal on my neck and my head fell into my green curry. It was getting too much for the men in white coats, they weren't doctors, just men in white coats. Apparently it was costing more in hush money for the people that I'd mentally scarred than it had been to keep me in the research unit. I was told to find something where all I did was sit, nothing strenuous, nothing that would make me lose my head.

There are all kinds of groups and meetings and sessions for folks to get things off their chest, even if that is where I went wrong in the first place. Although finding a group for the terminally headless was going to be difficult, I wanted something more bespoke but beggars can't be choosers. I decided to turn up at half seven on a Tuesday night and go with the flow, no matter what kind of ailment the group was for.

'Hello, my name is Gareth and I am an alcoholic.'

Well, it's a start and it isn't too far from the truth.

Andy Rivers

Andy is worried that our publication of his debut crime fiction novel, *'Maxwell's Silver Hammer'* in July, combined with his recent discovery of Kiwi fruit and Cous-Cous might turn him into one of those poncy middle-class author types.

Quick, someone get him a Greggs Pastie...

Daddy's Gone

'Bastard'

Caught me jumper on the fucking broken glass. I've been in and out of places like these loads of times and now I'm making mistakes like that - fucksakes. Mind, it's not like I've left any evidence is it? Bit of cotton on the glass - ooh I hope CSI Byker divvent get hold of that - as if.

The warehouse is dark and quiet. Not like this through the day mind - proper fuckin' busy then but not at night - not now. No nightshift anymore, all laid off last month see.

I'm down from the window, through the Goods In office and on the floor. That was a canny tip from Choker about the alarms an all, I wouldn't have touched a place like this if I didn't know they didn't work properly. He's worked here nearly five years has the big lad - straight from school onto nights in this dump. It was handy though what with me working nights as well - well you do in my trade divvent you - meant we could have a few bevvies through the day and that. Cos his dad was the supervisor it wasn't the end of the world if he turned up a few sheets to the wind - they soon learned to keep him off the forklift when that was the case - that dent's still in the wall look.

Aye, Choker's dad was a canny bloke. Always looked after me when I was a kid. When the rest of our class were getting picked up in Beamers and Mercs by their old men I'd be proper embarrassed some times but then the Cartwright wagon would turn up and I'd be hauled in. It was a bit like that Rolf Harris song really - you kna that bit 'did you think I would leave you lying there?' He used to buy us clothes an all. If he took Choker shopping for some new gear he'd always buy me a shirt or summit so I didn't feel left out - never made a big deal of it neither like some would of.

Me and Choker were top pals at school like. He was bigger than every fucker else, got his nickname when some posh fucker was taking the piss out of me. Asking us if I knew what '*bastard*' meant - course I knew I heard it every fucking day - anyways Choker grabbed him round the neck and told him he better say sorry. The kid wouldn't at first and then he couldn't cos he had no wind left in his pipe, hence 'Choker' - he's never shook it off to this day. After that people at school started using the nickname I had at home - 'Snake Simmons' as in built like a racing one. Aye, I'm a skinny fucker me - handy for getting in and out of windows like.

It was always useful at the match an' all, you kna when they had the old turnstiles and the terracing. Choker's dad would be paying at the window and I'd be under the gate and in. He'd get us both Bovril and a hot dog at half time and let us both run loose amongst the barriers. Fucking brilliant in them days man. Big George Reilly scoring that goal against Liverpool - all the jocks in the Gallowgate End were going mental that time. Choker's dad was mortal on the bus back. He kept saying how much he hated his boss and then ruffling both our heads telling us to stick in at school and show the world what we could do. I fuckin' hated his boss an' all mind but not enough to make me stick in at school...heh heh.

Where's them computer games then? This torch is fucked. Ah there we gan, battery's kicked in again. That looks like the fellas over there. Belter, fill me bag, out the window, back to bed. Sweet as.

It was a right bad time for the family when Choker's dad got the push last year mind. Times were hard in their house. He'd worked here all his life an' all and they just said he was surplus to requirements and hoyed him out the door with a statutory redundancy - wasn't enough to buy a fucking round in the boozer. Fucking tossers.

Choker was beside hisself at the funeral, hardly touched his beer and that. Blamed the company for it obviously, said they'd broke the old mans' heart and basically killed him the day they sacked him. I had to agree like. I mean they didn't put the rope round his neck or owt but they took away his reason for being here didn't they?

I decided then I was going to do the place over - get some of the money back they didn't give him when they got rid like. Thought I'd give it to Choker's mam what with her looking after us an' all when I was a kid. I mean me mam did her best but after the old fella walked out on her for a younger model she fell apart a bit. I still visit her in the hospital now and then but she doesn't kna it's me.

Aye, so I thought I'd weigh in for the funeral and that, mebbe's help out round theirs but it was too late. She couldn't live without him and we were at another one a week later.

Fuck it - can't dee nowt about it now. Bag's full so where'd I leave that petrol? Here we are then, the boardroom. Splash a bit here and a bit there. Keep the other can for the chairman's office - that's the fucker there with the brass plate on.

> **CEO - Mr. J. Simmons**

Right where's me matches...here we go, I've waited all me life for this. This one's for you Mr. Cartwright...and for me.

Keith Gingell

Keith is still a young bloke in an old man's body which is even bloody older now. He's not a Grumpy Old Man, but he's quite prepared to be if the BBC pay him enough. Despite his publishing success in Radgepacket 3 he hasn't let it go to his head, although he's a bit pissed off that English Heritage won't let him bolt a blue plaque onto his caravan in Southend.

Repo

'Here comes the sun king .... Everybody's happy, everybody's laughing.'

Jason stirred under his 13-TOG duvet. The bulge of his body moved, but not the tangle of brown hair sticking out like the trimmed fronds of a large carrot. A few seconds later an arm slid out and his hand groped the clock-radio.

'Here comes the sun king....'

Jason's torso breached the duvet, his eyes squinting from the light of the first-day-of-the-rest-of-his-life. Remembering the new 'my music' ring-tone he'd downloaded last night, he lunged at his Samsung.

'Everybody's happ- '

'Hello? . . . Hello?'

He fumbled the cover open. The phone confirmed, in white on orange, he'd missed a call. He pushed the view button. The same colours explained it was from Mandy Connell: his boss. A push on the green icon got her back in less than half a minute.

'Yes?'

'Did I wake you up?'

No. I was giving Angelina Jolie one before sending her back to Brad.

'Yes. As a matter-of-fact you did.' He noticed the time: 8.14am.'You're up early.'

'You're up late.' Mandy always answered accusation with accusation.

'I'm on afternoons today. Remember?'

'You think I'd forget?'

'Not really.'

'I've got an urgent job for you.'

'Now?'

'Yesterday.'

'What's up?'

'We had two repos arrive last night. I want them valued by this afternoon.'

Repos. Jason hated valuing repossessions. Sifting through other people's misery depressed him. With so many flooding in, doubly so. 'What's the rush? Anyway, where's Kate?

'She's been transferred to the West Park office.'

Lay-offs. The market was flat. 'Tim's gone then?'

'How should I know.'

Lying bitch.

'So what's the rush? It's only repos.'

The bank wants them sold quick. They didn't specify a lower limit. I want to get some offers in ASAP, before they change their minds.'

'Ah, Commission.'

'Commission for the company.'

Besides being a regular estate agents, the company specialised in handling bank repossessions. They always got first refusal. Mandy never refused.

'Which bank?'

'The Spanish outfit. Can you go? I'll make it up to you.'

'Make it up to you,' meant getting to keep his job a bit longer. 'I need to go to Tesco first, there's nothing in the house.'

'There's a Tesco's round the corner from one of them. You can leave it till last, then go get your ready-made Rogan Josh, or whatever you bachelors eat, when you've finished.'

Fuck you, Mandy.

'I don't eat ready-made, I cook everything from fresh, and Fifi's moving in this weekend.'

'Oh, good. That means you won't stink-out the office fridge with the smell of curry. And it's about time you married that girl.'

'You mean you want me to come to the office this aftern-?'

Silly question Jason.

'Okay Mandy, I'll be in about ten.'

'Try to make it nine-thirty, darlin'.'

'I'll do my best.'

'See you at nine-thirty, Jason.'

He closed his mobile, scratched his balls and threw back the duvet. Never work for a frigging woman.

Cruising slowly along High Street, Jason looked for a gap in the endless line of stationary vehicles. No luck. Goat Street car park again.

Grudgingly pushing a pound coin into the slot machine, he bought a self-adhesive ticket telling him he had till 10.23am before his time ran out. Always a quandary. Probably he'd be back in fifteen minutes and he'd have wasted fifty pence. On the other hand, Mandy might keep him talking and he'd have to run back to the car, sweating cobs, and move it or risk a £25 fine. Outside the display window, he checked his watch before pushing open the wide glass door of Johnson's Estates sales office:

9.29am.

'Morning Mandy.'

Looking up from her lap-top, she made a show of looking at the clock. 'Hmmm.'

She pointed to the chair in front of her desk with her index finger, its claw-like purple painted nail decorated with a gold lotus motif. Jason sat down, and picked up the envelope that lay in front of him. It contained a letter with the addresses of the properties and two multimap printouts which Mandy had prepared. He knew the areas: a Victorian terrace in a danger-ous corner of town - the last time he'd been there it'd cost him two years off his no-claims bonus and his insurance company a paint job - and a newish detached on a fashionable middle class development, as Mandy said, five minutes drive from a superstore.

Today, his boss wore a beige suede jacket, unbuttoned over a low neck bottle green cotton jumper. He concentrated on not glancing at the tops of her ample, forty-five year-old breasts. She peered into his eyes over her Gucci readers, a smirk on her face. She knew he would break and look down eventually. She knew she was fit.

He felt inside the envelope. 'Where's the keys?' he said, holding her gaze.

Mandy leaned back, her cleavage shifted sensuously.

Jason broke.

She smiled; he blushed.

'A courier's bringing them. Should be here in about fifteen minutes. Coffee?'

He managed a nod. 'I'll get them,' he said getting to his feet, glad of the chance to look away.

'No. It's alright. I'll do it. You'd better get the camera.'

She stood up and headed to the back of the office where the coffee machine was kept. Her chocolate brown skirt clung to her swaying roundness. Jason watched her for about five seconds, then went over to the filing cabinet where the company's Nikon was kept.

Better check the battery and memory card. It wouldn't be the first time he'd arrived at a valuation, only to find the first was empty and the second was full. He switched the camera on and squinted through the viewfinder. The icons indicated the batteries were healthy and the memory card quarter full. He panned around and caught Mandy in the frame as she bent down to place a tray on her desk. The auto-focus sharpened her image.

'Don't you dare.'

Click.

'Just testing it.' Jason looked at the image and raised his eyebrows. 'Nice.'

'You'd better delete that.'

'It's a good one. Look,' he said and handed the machine over.

Mandy took the Nikon, her expression scolding. Her features softened when she peered at the viewer. She saw herself gazing back, captured in the gentle morning light. Her blonde-grey hair cascading across her face. And that cleavage. She looked fifteen years younger. It was very flattering. And if there was one thing Mandy liked; it was flattery.

She's laughing, she's actually laughing.

It was more of a girlish giggle. She gave the camera back.

'Just delete it.' But her sparkling eyes were saying, 'keep it.'

'Don't you want it for your desktop?'

'Maybe I'll-'

'Mizz Connell?'

She looked over to the door. 'Yes?'

'TNT. Delivery.'

Flirting over, Mandy was Mandy again as she walked up to the skinny youth in an orange jacket. His head was encased in a beach-ball sized crash-helmet, making him look top-heavy.

'Sign here Ma'am.' He stared at her tits, while she focused on his clipboard and signed a paper.

She returned it, tipping her head to one side: her sideways look telling him she knew he was staring, but didn't care.

'Thanks.'

He avoided her eyes and handed her an A4 padded envelope. He said a muffled, 'See you,' from behind his helmet and left as quietly as he came.

Cheeky little bugger.

She sashayed to her desk and passed the envelope to Jason.

He opened it and tipped the contents onto the desk. Two bunches of keys fell out, each labelled with an address. The pair busied themselves separating the keys, labelling fobs and drinking coffee. When they finished, Jason took two fobs - each with three keys attached - and put them in his envelope.

'You'd better stop by Stanhope's and get another set of copies cut - just in case.'

'Okay.'

'Don't forget to get a receipt.'

At five quid a key d'you think I'd forget ?

'No, I won't.'

Jason finished his coffee, packed everything in his pilot's case and left the sales office. He returned to his car at 10.17am, pleased he'd not wasted his pound.

Number Forty Seven, Rose Street stood about third of the way along a narrow street with an unbroken terrace of flat-fronted Victorian houses on each side. The overcast grey sky added to its dismal atmosphere. It was like being in a tunnel with the roof removed.

Some of the frontages were in excellent condition, displaying the original red brickwork. Others had been re-faced by proud owners in varying degrees of kitsch.

Number Forty Seven, however, was none of these. It was suffering. The paint had peeled into bare holes, the pointing had gaps up to a foot long in places. The hundred-and-twenty year old stone lintels were pockmarked; one was cracked. Remnants of broken tiles from the roof lay in the gutter.

Jason groaned as he pulled his car up in front of it. It was risky parking here, but he figured at this time of the morning the kids from the area would either be in school or glue sniffing in a public toilet somewhere.

Barge-pole job. She'd be crazy to put this on the books. He took his case from the car, put his overcoat on, locked the car and double checked all the doors. After a final glance to make sure he'd left nothing in view, he approached the scarred front door and tried one of the Yale keys in the grubby lock.

The door opened with a squawk of damp wood rubbing against damp doorframe. The dim carpet-less hallway led to a naked flight of stairs. Turning into the living room, Jason nearly tripped over a filthy wine coloured carpet that had been pulled away from the wall and lay in upside-down folds. He smiled a knowing smile to himself as he smelled a familiar smell. A mixture of stale beer, piss and marijuana. This place had been no, 'home-sweet-home.' There were a lot of these in this area.

To Jason, repos fell into two categories: either left tidy by sad ex-owners, reluctant to leave the home they'd sacrificed everything to buy, or angry ones who left revengeful damage for the banks to repair. The occupants of Forty Seven had been very enthusiastic examples of the latter. Every panel of every door had several Doc Martin sized holes in it. The oven was in pieces, the door of the fridge hung open on one twisted hinge, exposing its mould infested interior. Hammer holes peppered those doors still on the kitchen cupboards. He made his way to the scullery, wondering if, like so many Victorian houses, it had been converted into a downstairs bathroom. It had. He placed a pre-emptory hand over his nose and opened the door. It was clean and tidy. Oh, so girls also lived here. Returning to the kitchen, he noticed the cellar door. Jason decided to make a quick tour of the upper floor to get the layout of the place.

'Fifty grand top-whack,' he said out loud, as he climbed the stairs. 'And another fifty to get this place habitable. Even Martin Roberts'd turn his nose up at this one.'

The rooms upstairs were no surprise. Two large doubles. One was clean - ish. Someone had painted the walls purple and it had a carpet. The girl's room. The other: filthy. Pornographic posters had been glued directly onto ancient flowery wall paper. The bailiffs had made a half-hearted attempt at removing a couple before giving up. The boy's room. The third room, a small one, was totally bare. It didn't look like it was used for sleeping. Jason confirmed this when he noticed a used syringe, complete with needle, wedged in the gap between two floor boards. Those lazy fuckers are supposed to clean places like this before we get the keys. The view of the short back-yard from the rear window, showed a tumble-down outhouse and a mass of tangled weeds and a couple of grass engulfed supermarket trolleys. Eat your heart out Diarmuid Gavin.

Back in the living room, Jason rummaged in his case for a flash-light. Reluctantly, he opened the cellar and shone the beam into it. It was surprisingly clean and bright. The walls were whitewashed and no rats scuffled away. He carefully descended the stairs, waving the flash-light around. At the bottom, he saw the gas meter on the far corner. Facing him, an old-fashioned fuse box. It hung squiffily, a little bit away from the bricks. It looked unsafe. Re-wiring job. He crossed for a closer look. When he touched the casing, the whole unit tipped forward. Behind it was a deep hole where some bricks had been removed.

A plastic bag crammed with skunk florets, six large slabs of resin wrapped in foil, and a pile of baggies with white powder in them confronted Jason.

In a strange way, he felt relieved as he climbed out of the cellar, knowing there would be no more valuing repos today. Well, Mandy. That's your plans buggered up. When he had a signal on his mobile, he clicked 'contacts' and scrolled down to the office number.

The line rang seven times before his boss answered. 'Hello, Johnson's Estates,' she sang, 'one moment please.'

'Are you with a client?'

'Hello, Jason.'

'I'm at Rose Street. We have a problem. You'd better go to the private phone.'

'Oh? Can you tell me what it is?' Her tone of voice made it clear she was with a client.

'Down in the cellar, I found enough dope to knock out a herd of elephants.'

'I'll have to put you on hold. One moment Jason.'

The hold music told him she was making her excuses and handing over to the part-time girl. After about a minute he heard the line click.

'Jason. Just do as I say. Get out of there now and go over to the other house. When you finish, go back to Rose Street and call the police.'

'You're kidding right? This place is a fucking crime scene.'

'Don't use that kind of language to me.'

'What you're asking me to do is illegal, Mandy.'

'Nobody will know.'

'The police aren't that bloody stupid. They'll be asking difficult enough questions as it is. There's a lot of gear here. If they find out I was here twice, they're gonna crucify me.'

'If it gets difficult, I'll explain. I'll take full responsibility. Jason. . . . Please. I won't let you get into trouble.'

'Shit, Mandy!'

'You'll be okay, I promise. Just get out of there. NOW.'

He knew he should refuse. They couldn't fire him for refusing to do something illegal. At least, not straight away. But there again, he'd have something over the firm if things got tough.

'Alright.'

He closed the mobile and put it in his overcoat pocket. Taking one final look around, he gathered up his things and left the house.

The clouds had broken up. Rose Street, brightened by the

late winter-sun, looked almost cheerful. Jason's car sat in its glare and the interior was warming up. He placed his pilot case in the passenger foot-well and removed his overcoat, laying it carefully on the rear seat. He wasted no further time belting-up and driving off.

Bloody Mandy. It's alright for her.

If the police get wind of this, she isn't the one who's going to get questioned and accused and belittled by those suspicious bastards all fucking night.

By the time Jason reached the suburb of North Compton on the other side of town, he'd calmed down. He pulled up on the drive-way of Fifteen, Osprey Gardens. It stood, partially hidden by shrubbery in the corner of a cul-de-sac on the Eagle Estate. All the streets were named after raptors. He scanned the beige-bricked four-bedroom detached house. This is more like it. Nice place - be a miracle to find anything dodgy in here. He sat in the car while he sorted out the keys to the house.

He took his case and stepped out the car. Outside, he felt the unseasonable warmth of the sun on his face and decided to leave his coat behind. It's safe there. He stretched and looked around, assessing the area. A dormitory street, I doubt there'll be anybody here much before five.

Turning towards the property he intended to enter, he baulked. Something wasn't quite right, but he couldn't finger it. Debating whether to take the photo while the sun shone, he stared a full minute across at the house and neat lawn - That's it; the grass . . . strange.

It was mid-February - two days after St. Valentines - nobody cut their grass now, even in the South. This was the cooler, East Midlands. But the lawn was trimmed: cropped close, almost like a putting green. Jason frowned, puzzled by the knowledge that the place had stood empty for weeks. He shrugged, and let himself into the property.

Immediately, he began to feel uncomfortable. The hall had an atmosphere. A smell of perfume. Not women's perfume, Chanel Number 5 or men's after-shave, like Paco Rabanne.

Detergents: cleaners.

Jason detected lavender, pine and rose, as if someone had just finished spring cleaning. The smell persisted in the lounge - stronger even. The expensive parquet floor gleamed and the smell of wax joined in with the others. A symphony of essences invaded his nostrils.

In seven years surveying and valuing property, he couldn't say how many repos he'd done. A lot. What he could say: he'd never been in one like this. Nobody left them this clean. Jason passed through the lounge and entered the kitchen. Same thing. Everything perfect; no dust, no cooking deposits. He'd seen dirtier show houses. The place seemed inhabited.

Impossible.

To make sure it wasn't, he checked the water and power. They were locked off. He breathed a sigh of relief.

The cupboards were empty, the insides cleaner than the day they were installed. Jason bent to open the one under the sink. He jumped back as if he'd received a 240 volt jolt.

What the Hell?

He stared at the neat line of cleaning products. Bleach, toilet cleaner, Mr. Sheen, oven cleaner, wood polish. It was all there. Next to it lay a pile of cloths, two rolls of patterned kitchen paper, house gloves and four, five-litre containers of water. Also a pack of refuse bags.

Something was seriously bizarre.

Bloody hell, someone's got a key! I'll have to call Mandy.

Feeling in his jacket pocket, he remembered his mobile in the car.

Jesus, what else can go wrong today.

'What are you doing in my house?'

Jason whirled round. A man glared at him from the kitchen entrance. He wore a blue shirt, brown cord trousers and tweed jacket, but they seemed crumpled. In fact, the man's face looked crumpled too - everything about him just looked crumpled. Like a crisp bag that re-opens itself after it's been screwed up. The man didn't look like a squatter. Not threatening. No face piercing, no pink Mohawk or tattooed skin-head dome. Jason took a deep breath and spoke, choosing his words carefully. 'I don't think you are supposed to be in here, sir.'

'What do you mean? I live here.' The man thrust his hands into his jacket pockets. 'I- I've lived here for f-four years. Ever since this place was built. . . . When I bought it.'

Jason's training never included this. Squatters yes. And he'd forgotten the basic rules: always keep an eye out for squatter activity before entering a property. Always keep a mobile with you. He could feel his pulse racing as he searched for something to say.

Smiling, he said, 'Um, I think there must be some mistake. I need to make a call. My mobile's in my car. Excuse me.' He moved towards the kitchen door, but the man made no attempt to stand aside.

He glanced down a Jason's shoes. 'You've made the floor dirty with your feet. You did that in the lounge too.' The floor was clean. 'You'll have to go in the garage while I clean this mess up for Sandra.' He pointed to a door next to the fridge-freezer.

'Sandra?'

The man didn't seem to hear. 'Please go into the garage, I- I have to clean.' He leaned over and opened the connecting door into the garage. 'Please.'

'Sorry, but I need to get my mobile.' Jason tried to dart into the lounge.

The man jumped back, blocking the door. 'No, no, no. You'll make it dirty for Sandra.' He stepped forward and grabbed Jason's shoulder, catching him off-balance, and pushed him into the garage.Struggling to stay upright, Jason stepped backward a few paces. He stood in the centre of the spotless garage floor. He was afraid, but also pissed-off.

'You can't do this. The house isn't yours now. The bank's reposse...'

'The bank? You're from the bank!' The man's face turned red, his eyes wild. Then he lunged forward.

Jason never saw the knife, but he felt a searing pain in the side of his neck as the force of the blow knocked him to the floor. He landed on his back. He rolled over onto his side and tried to push himself up. His arm didn't work. He tried to shout: his voice didn't work. He felt suddenly tired and laid his head on the cold cement. The regular pattern of bricks and mortar filled his field of vision. Something warm was moving around his cheek, heating up the floor.

What happened . . .?

What's going . . . on?

Oh God, I think I've been st...

The bricks merged into a terracotta blur.

Then.

Nothing.

The man stepped back and looked down at his trousers, spattered with Jason's blood.

'I'm sorry Sandra,' he mumbled, 'I won't leave the house dirty again. I promise.'

Stepping away from the path of blood running to the drain in the centre of the garage, he knelt. He loosened his shoes and removed them. He stripped completely naked and made a tidy pile of his clothes - except for his shirt which he used to wipe blood off his hands and face. He returned to the kitchen, closed the door to the garage and took some cleaning materials from the cupboard.

It took him an hour to clean the kitchen and polish the fifty square metres of parquet in the lounge. He replaced the cleaning materials in the kitchen, stored Jason's case in the pantry and shuffled back to the hall with a duster under each foot. Still naked, he stood on the threshold of the entrance connecting the hallway to the lounge.

'Just as you like it Sandra. It'll be perfect for you when you come to see me.'

Upstairs, in the empty main bedroom, there were four indentations in the deep pile of the blue carpet, marking an oblong space where a bed once stood. The naked man, spotless kitchen knife in hand, crossed the room and sat down inside the space.

Using information he'd read in a detective novel six months ago - When things were good. Before the bank took everything away. Before Sandra and the kids left with that financial advisor -The man dug the knife into his left arm.

When he found the main artery, he gritted his teeth and carefully drew the tip up his arm opening a four inch gash.

'Goodbye Sandra.'

He lay in the puddle of his blood, rapidly spreading across the carpet and closed his eyes: his lips formed a serene smile.

In the office Mandy was getting impatient.

'Jason should be back at Rose Street by now. Why the bloody hell does he always wait for me to call him?'

She pushed, 'Jason' on her auto-dial.

Inside the pocket of the coat in Jason's car, the screen on his mobile lit up.

'Here comes the sun king . . . Everybody's happy, everybody's laughing. . . .'

Paul Brazill

Paul D. Brazill was born in Hartlepool - a town famous for hanging a monkey - and is now on the lam in Poland. His stories have appeared both online and in print. His column *'I didn't say that, did I?'* is a regular sore spot at Pulp Metal Magazine, you can find his musings on life, lager and everything at http://pdbrazill.blogspot.com

The Night Watchman

A Peter Ord Investigation.

Paddy's had more birthdays than the Queen. He's sat at the bar in The Raby Arms wearing his beer stained Concorde Security Services uniform, head wobbling around like one of those little toy dogs that people used to have in the back of their cars in the sixties and fiddling with an unlit Embassy cigarette. As the afternoon staggers on, he's getting more and more wound up.

'It's bad enough having to work on me birthday,' he says 'And me a pensioner ... but when I can't even have a tab in the pub ...on me birthday.'

His face is like a blackcurrant crumble and so lived-in, squatters wouldn't stay there. He keeps jabbing the cigarette to accentuate each point, like he's about to throw a dart.

'Gotta work, haven't I?' Says Paddy. 'Birthday or not. Haven't got two pennies to rub together, have I? Pensioner, aren't I?'

The Raby Arms, like most of its punters, is permanently nicotine stained and it'll take more than a few years of a smoking ban to cleanse it of its faggy tinge. Like most afternoons, it's half empty - worse since the Wetherspoons pub opened down the road - and most of the customers are old school friends of Methuselah, nursing half pints of Strongarm and waiting for someone to buy them a drink. Behind the bar today is Sleepy Jim, who usually works at Velvettes Gents' Club. At the moment he's filling in for Cameron, the usual barman, and Sleepy's not too happy about it.

'Don't get me wrong, Peter,' says Sleepy, 'sometimes the crack's good but, you know, at least at Velvettes I get a flash of gash and even the odd tip. Most of the punters are out of towners on business trips. Here, I'm like the kid in that Bruce Willis film. I see dead people.'

'So what's the problem with Cameron?' I say.

'Best not ask,' says Sleepy, wiping his glasses with his tie. 'Lets just say, if he shows his face around here again, it'll be missing a nose. If Jack's got anything to do with it..'

I sip my pint of Stella. Jack Martin, the owner of both The Raby Arms and Velvettes Gents' Club is not someone to cross. Paddy turns and looks at me.

'It's me birthday, y'know,'he says.

'Many happy returns. Time flies,' I say. 'It's come around so soon'

Sleepy smirks as he puts in a CD.

'Gladys Shite and The Pimps, eh?' I say as '*Midnight Train To Georgia*'creeps out of the tiny sound system.

I nod to Sleepy Jim. 'Get him whatever he's drinking, Jim.'

Paddy grins. 'Cheers, brother. You're a gentleman and a scholar.'

I glance at my reflection in the mirror behind the bar and think that maybe I look like a gentleman or a scholar. I can see a bespectacled man in a sober suit. A chief accountant, maybe, a CFED teacher or a low rent solicitor, but certainly not a Private Investigator.

Paddy looks up at the clock, downs the pint of Stella and the Bell's chaser in no time and staggers off the stool.

'Off to graft now,' he says. 'On me friggin birthday.' He bumps into me and slowly squints at me like he's trying to scrutinise a magic eye painting.

'Scuse me brother, do I know you?' .

'Only for about fifteen years, Paddy,' I say. ' Been a lot of booze under the bridge since then, though, eh? I'm Peter. Peter Ord.'

'Ord,' he says, looking around the room for help. 'I know that name...'

An invisible light bulb appears above his head.

'Aahaa! You're the private dickhead that Olly's missus paid to follow him. See if he was banging birds during night shift.'

'Strictly confidential, Paddy,' I say.

'Aye. Well, he was better off shot of her, brother. She'd had enough cock to make a handrail round the QE2, I can tell you.'

The old grandfather clock in the corner strikes two and Paddy reacts like a prize fighter.

'Frigging 'ell. Two o'clock. Gotta start me shift, brother.'

As he stumbles out of the room I wave to him.

'Happy Birthday, Paddy.'

He pauses, the door half open, letting in the warm, summer air.'Birthday,' he says, perplexed.

'It's not me friggin' birthday until May.'

*****

When I think about it, my most vivid and powerful memories of childhood are in black and white. The monochrome of the Saturday morning Odeon's Kidz-Klub, and the Hollywood films on afternoon television, seemed so much more vibrant than anything that real life could come up with. And, as you would expect of someone who grew up living more fully in his imagination than in the day-to-day, adulthood proved to be a series of disappointments and non-events.

So, when I decided to become a Private Investigator, although I certainly didn't have any romantic illusions that the job would bear any resemblance to the lives of Messrs Marlowe and Spade, I had, a least, a smattering of hope that there may be a little silver screen glamour to the job. Over the years, however, that hope and I have barely been on nodding terms.

So, when I walk into Jack Martin's suffocating red leather and oak office at Velvette's Gentleman's Club. I'm not exactly expecting to be hired to find the Rara Avis. Still...

'A babysitter?' I say?

Jack glares at me, blue eyes piercing beetroot skin.

'You used to be a teacher, right?' he says, filling two tumblers with brandy, his voice bearing more than a passing resemblance to that of the tiger in The Jungle Book..

'Once upon a time,' I say.

'English?'says Jack

I think of the staff room at Dyke House School stuffed with disappointment and cigarette smoke and am immediately draped in a cloak of gloom. I gulp my brandy.

'English Lit, I believe ?' says Jack, lighting a King Edward cigar.

I nod.

'Right, well. Listen. My little angel, Holly, is doing her A Levels at the mo and isn't doing so well at the subject. Can't tell King Lear from a pig's ear . The lives of dead poets hold bugger all interest to her. So,well, I've decided that you can give her a little extra tutorial, while I'm away in Lansagrotty.'

'But why me? There must be lots of eager ...'

Jack holds up a hand.

'Yes, well, maybe too eager, some of them,' he says. 'Holly's a beautiful young girl and I don't want anyone trying to have their wicked way with her. She needs to concentrate on her studies. Her future. So, yes, as well as helping with her stanzas and whatnot you can keep an eye out for any unsavoury characters. You'll be like a nightwatchman.'

Just like Paddy, I think. I shuffle in my seat.

'So, the English lessons are just a cover?' I say.

'Not much gets past you, lad,' says Jack. 'I know she's safe with you. She wouldn't touch you with Roman Polanski or any other five foot Pole.'

He chuckles to himself, picks up a copy of the Times and starts on the crossword. Nothing like an ego boost to start the day.

*****

It's Saturday night and I'm nestled on a bar stool contemplating the evening's third double whisky, the ice cubes shimmering, glimmering and glowing in the wan light.

Uncharacteristically, The Raby Arms is heaving and, unfortunatley, so is the man next to me.

'Paddy, watch what you're doing,' I say, stepping away from the pool of pavement pizza.

'Sorry, brother,' says Paddy.

I move closer to the bar. Sleepy is in full on seventies disco mode, playing Sheila & B. Devotions' 'Spacer' much to the chagrin of the cast of 'Cocoon' that are stuffed into the far corner of the room.

The rest of the customers, a bunch of sweaty Muscle Marys

on their way to Newcastle to see Shirley Bassey, seem happy enough though.

'So, Sleepy. You've worked for Jack Martin for as long as I can remember.Tell me about Holly.'

'Spoilt little twat, if you ask me.Worse since Mrs Martin popped her clogs, God rest her soul. She looks like butter wouldn't melt in her mouth but I've heard that a few chav stiffies have. They don't call her Minstrels for nothing.'

'Oh, great.'

'Yeah,' says Sleepy 'And I've also heard she's got a thing for older men. So you better watch your step.'

Suddenly, someone bangs into me and I spill my beer. I turn and see Paddy swaying toward me.

'Ey, you're him. The gumshoe?' he says. I recoil from his acid breath.

'Just the man I need,' says Paddy.

'Yeah?' I say.

'Yeah. Listen....' he drags me toward a small table in the corner.

'I was on the force, you know, for twenty years, man and boy. In uniform the whole time. I worked on the lot. Even murder.. Even the Binns' fur robbery. Remember that?'

Who could forget. A bunch of Braniacs in the Seventies broke into the department store warehouse and stole a fair amont of expensive mink coats. Unfortunately, they used a Robin Reliant as a getaway car and so it didn't exactly take Columbo to track them down since about one million people noticed the car crawling down the street.

'My best mate, Starskey to my Hutch, was a bloke called Ernie Teal. Side by side we were. Me and my shadow, like Flannagan and Allen. Well. He made Detective and moved down south to Dar..Dar..'

'Dartford?' I said.

'Naw, Darlington. Or York. Somewhere like that. Anyway, he disappeared into thin air.. we were like blood brothers, we were...'

'And so you want me to track him down?'

'Indeed, brother, ' says Paddy, 'ex-copper - shouldn't be too

hard, eh ...? And I know you'll have connections. In the force.'
    I drain my glass.
    'Another pint of Nelson?' I say to Paddy.
    'Aye,' he splutters.
    The misconception that Paddy had is a common one. Lots
of people think that PI's are ex-cops with connections in the
police force and the underworld. And maybe that's true of
some of them but in my cases I have to use other resources. In
the case of tracking down Detective Sergent Ernest Teal, well,
I'm going to use something called the Yellow Pages.

                            *****

    The evening is melting into night and dark, malignant
clouds are spreading themselves across the sky. I pull down
the metal shutters and lock up Las Vegas Amusements - my
main source of income -as a battered yellow taxi cab splutters
to a halt in front of the arcade.
    The deodorant soaked taxi snakes it's way along the sea
front, past pubs, greasy spoons, gift shops and amusement
arcades, as the rain falls down in sheets. It heads outside the
town, behind the park, where the buses don't run, towards a
six bedroom mock Tudor house perched on the hill, looming
over the town like a great black bat. The taxi stutters to a full
stop outside a swinging sign: 'Dun Robbin.'
    The door is opened by a petite, short-haired blonde in a
Cradle Of Filth t-shirt and cut off jeans so tight you can read
her lips. And she is stunning. My jaw drops so much that you
could scrape carpet fluff from my bottom lip.
    'Holly?' I say.
    'Follow me, Mr. Teacher,' she says and she leads me into a
house too kitsch for Liberace. .
    'Help yourself to a drink,' says Holly 'And I'll slip into
something more comfortable.'And, as she goes upstairs, I do
just that. I pour myself a large Zubrowka and apple juice and
head towards trouble like dirty dishwater down a plughole.
    After a minute, dressed exactly the same, Holly is down the
stairs with a pile of books and next to me on the sofa.

'This is cosy, isn't it?' she says. I swig the vodka to wash away the dark and dingy thoughts that are lurking in the murky corners of my mind and immediately, an old Police song corkscrews through my brain. And I friggin' hate Sting.

*****

Early morning and the air tastes like lead and the sky is gun metal grey as the big black Grand Central train pulls into the station. I'm overwhelmed with a sense of foreboding. Maybe it's foreshadowing or maybe it's just the hangover. I take a seat and pull out a copy of '*Saturday Night, Sunday Morning*' it's at least a couple of hours to York.

I try to concentrate on the book but end up gazing out of the window at the rows of concrete blocks being smudged by the morning rain and end up nodding off. When I peel back my eyelids, the sunlight stings my eyes and I see that the train is pulling into York Station.

From the photos it looks as if Ernie Teal was an oak of a man, and you could easily imagine him overpowering the various ne'er-do-wells that he came across before he took early retirement. Mrs Rose Teal was, and still is, a stumpy woman, however, who seems out of sorts without her husband.

'He just scarpered,' she says, sitting with her handbag on her knee, clasping the handle with both hands.

'Any indication as to ...' I start to say.

'Oh, he blamed it on the house, said it was draining money. He was against moving here, really. Gentrification he called it but then, he never liked Yorkshire. Said it were full of homosexuals.' She sips her tea.

'He left me well provided for, though. I'll give him that. Paid for the mortgage and left a lot of money in the bank.Then he just buggered off to Brazil.'

At once, my spider senses start tingling. Corruption, payoffs, bribery. This is it, I think. A real case: bent copper pisses off to South America with a well stacked ...

'I reckon he'd have stayed if he hadn't won the lottery.'

'What?' I say 'Lottery?'

'Oh aye. Eight million quid, near as dammit. Blessing and a curse.'

Awkwardly, I dip my custard cream into my tea and just stare as it crumbles onto the coffee table when I take it out.

*****

'You did well, lad,' says Jack, his skin looking weirdly bronzed. 'After that.... faux pas ... you had with that lapdancer last year, I wasn't 100% sure that you could be trusted but ...well, the CCTV speaks for itself.'

Jack started counting out the wad of cash.

'I could see it all. The only visitor my angel had was that Carole girl from school. And they just stayed in her room studying until the early hours, not even a trip to a nightclub.'

As I put the money into my jacket pocket I flash back to the night, I fell asleep drunk on the sofa at Jack's house. This segues into me going looking for the toilet, accidentally walking into Holly's bedroom and finding her and Carole involved in what the tabloids would call 'Girl On Girl Love Action'or 'vagitarianism'. I fade out as I close the door, unseen.

'Let's hope she passes her exams,' I say, finishing off my brandy.

Jack grins.

'No need to worry about that, he says. 'The head of the local education department is a regular in Velvettes. He owes me big time after a recent ... indescretion.'

'It's not what you know, it's who you know,' I say.

*****

'Gripping this, eh?' I say, but Sleepy Jim is enthralled, staring at the television screen. 'Deal or no Deal,' does that to some people.

The door bursts open and Paddy wanders in, his flies as wide as the Grand Canyon. He staggers toward the toilet.

'Oh, Paddy,' I say. 'I've got some news for you. Sort of good news and bad news.'

'What's that, then, brother,' says Paddy, jiggling around a little.

'It's about that mate of yours,' I say. I tracked him down. I know where he is but the expenses it'll cost you for me to get to him might be a little more than you're willing to pay.' I smirk a little. 'He's in Brazil.'

Paddy has the toilet door almost open and he turns to look at me.

'Brazil? Who do I know in Brazil?'

'Ernie Teal, ' I say. 'Your old mate. Cagney to your Lacey.'

Paddy shakes his head.

'Ernie Teal? What would I want to see that tosser for? Never could stand the bloke.'

And he turns, farts, and stumbles into the toilets.

I finish my drink and see that Sleepy Jim is grinning.

'I reckon that's one you won't get paid for,' he says.

'Yep, I'll just have to put it down to experience,' I say.

Jim taps my empty pint glass. 'You want another one?'

'Well,' I say. 'In the absence of the stuff that dreams are made of, a pint of Stella will do very nicely indeed.'

<u>Andrew Kirby</u>

There's always one who goes too far, isn't there? We're talking pitch invasions at Subbuteo, stage-diving in Church, getting all pally with Les Dennis and scaring the man. When he isn't breaking laptops or falling asleep on trains, Andy tells stories. He's written four novels and many short pieces. Visit his website for more info
www.andykirbythewriter.20m.com

Background Noise

We reach the Church Hall, and it's all brightly lit already, and there's plenty of people milling uselessly about outside. Newton Mills is big on community and as soon as the doors of the Land Rover open, these zombies are on us, offering to help us carry in the equipment, asking if we want nice cups of tea and the like. I long to tell them all to fook off right there and then, but know that if I did, the chances of us even reaching the stage would be remote. I can't see the TV crews there yet, but Howard, Billy's dad, says he's called an old mate at Granada and called in a favour; he's convinced they're going to turn up to put this poxy charade on their Six O' Clock News programme. If they do, then maybe even the mighty Tony Wilson will see us...

We get out of the Land Rover and hand our worldly posses-sions over to these do-gooders... well, most of us do, but not Tunes. He looks at these weirdos like they're trying to nick his very soul and give it to some poor starving African kid when they try and take his guitar case from him. In the bright out-side lights of the Church Hall, he looks spookily white, and his angry spots shine out like Blackpool Illuminations on his boat.

Anyway, so the town Mayor comes up and mumbles some pleasantries to us, clearly with more than half a mind on the buffet that's probably inside. Funnily enough, Billy starts try-ing to engage him in a proper conversation, introducing each and every one of us with some stupid anecdote like he's the captain of a Second Division club that's somehow reached the FA Cup Final and the Mayor's Prince Charles.

'And I'm sure, lads, that you'll tone down the language to suit your audience. Remember, this is all to raise money for a new sixth form block,' mumbles the town Mayor, who looks as though he'd long to pepper his own speech with the odd swear. He'd love to be young enough, irresponsible enough to get away with it.

'We've come up with a special kind of show,' continues Billy, unabashed. 'It's different from what we usually do. It's more exciting.'

84

He's right, you know, Billy. We have come up with some-thing that'll blow the socks off some of these old bastards in the audience. I only hope that Granada are here to see it. Old Mayor though couldn't care less about what Billy has to say, and he's already sloping away, tapping his watch.

The Church Hall is a one-storey red-brick building which looks a bit like an extended old folk's bungalow. It reeks of that same tea and cress and disinfectant smell that those places have too. It's set just behind the church, handily overlooking the graveyard, just so it can remind the do-gooders what the end result of all of their pointless toil will be. I've been in here before, I think, probably at that fateful Jumble Sale where I sold all my Star Wars figures for the price of a few pints. What would they have been worth in a few years time if I'd have kept a hold of them? I shudder to think. Anyway, so the place has given me deep psychological scars, as it has Tunes, who used to be dragged here for Sunday School by his mam, when every-one else was turning tricks on their BMXs.

I'm behind Tunes as we push through the hospital-style double doors and enter the corridor which leads to the main room (operating theatre) and I see that flicker of apprehen-sion cross his face. Unfortunately for Tunes, if a flicker of apprehension crosses his face, it's a bit like shaking up a test tube that's got all sorts of volatile chemicals in it; as his brow trembles, toxic substances are released and explode on his face. His spots are like radioactive alarm signals. Once more, I thank fook that I was never cursed with the damn things.

I follow him as he shuffles into the entrance hallway, where Key-Ring and Billy are already stood talking to Do-Nowt. It looks like Do-Nowt has been put in charge of the door; which includes taking the money from the audience as they arrive. If there is anyone less suitable for this task in the whole of Newton Mills then show them to me; in fact, if there is anyone less suitable in the whole of the UK, then I'd quite like to know about how slippery that motherfooker would be.

Do-Nowt's sat down, of course, and doesn't look as though he'd be remotely bothered if anyone wanted to barge through without paying. Nah, he's too busy making little piles of what he's already taken: one for the school, two for me... two for the school, four for me. He's in his element, in as much as this lazy bastardo could ever look as though he would revel in anything. And the thing is, he lacks so much daisical that some dopey fooker would probably mistake him for a statue. And statues don't steal, do they?

Do-Nowt's sat in front of this big, luminous pink poster which says: 'Newton Mills Sixth Form Extravaganza', but in this shabby corridor, it looks out of place, like them pink socks city-types used to wear under their pin-striped suits. The poster's like modernity crashing in on the mothball-world of a dead kid's bedroom which has been kept exactly the same since they went and fooked off. I see Magnetic Fish Pond right down at the bottom of the bill (really the top) and realise that they are saving us for when most of the old folks have retired to bed for the evening with their cocoa and their detective novel which has a bit of racy sex in it, innit. I feel immense loathing being generated from within the marrow of my bones. As Howard said; we will 'tear this place apart.'

'We've got to sit through three hours of shit before we're on,' Billy says. 'They got the First Year girls starting the evening off with a dance show. Then we got speeches and that; the brass band...What they call a 'short intermission' - which probably means a piss stop for all the old grannies - and then it's the DJ. He's playing a sixties and seventies set... at a fundraising event for the Sixth Form.'

'Crap,' I agree.

'And then it's us. At about half ten...'

'Fook it,' I say, 'shall we fook off down the Peaks for a bit?'

Billy looks at me doubtfully for a minute - well, a second - and then just nods his head a bit sadly, resigned-like. Like he's just agreed that yeah, there is no choice, we'd have to lop his leg off to avoid the infection spreading. Key-Ring follows us, like a flapping ginger lap-dog, but Tunes is hanging back.

'What's up wiv you?' asks Do-Nowt in a way that implies that he's not particularly bothered about the answer. The only thing that's bothering him is if Tunes hangs about him like a particularly bad smell, drawing attention to his pilfering.

'You not joining your likkle chums?'

'No,' mutters Tunes, sounding embarrassed about some-thing. 'I thought I'd watch the performance. I wanted to see the brass band...'

'He fancies that bird with the jugs in the band,' moons Billy, as though describing a bird as 'the one with jugs' would automatically let us know who the fook he was on about.

'Which one, the one like this,' says Do-Nowt, actually doing the actions to accompany his speech - he motions, with spread hands, humongous tits, 'or the one like this?' And now he puts his two hands by his chest and extends the pointing fingers of each; massive erect nipples. We all know exactly who they are talking about now.

'It's nothing like that,' cries Tunes. 'I just enjoy all types of music.'

'Yer a soft-arse get,' says Key-Ring.

We wander away. I look back and see Tunes remonstrating with Do-Nowt some more. Key-Ring's right: he is a soft-arse. He's probably taken exception to Do-Nowt's 'objectification of women' or some such nonsense. So we fook him and go.

The Peaks is a short walk downhill from the Church Hall and, despite its prime location on the High Street, close to the train and bus stations, is as scruffy a place as you could possi-bly hope to see. They keep the lights on low here so you can't make out the shit on the carpet, but you feel it. You feel it grab-bing at your shoes as you walk through the door; sucking you in to this pit of despondency. The carpet is sticky from years of spilled beer, crisps, piss and vomit, but there's something else too. The carpet holds in it the shattered, big dreams of the landlord.

They once had big schemes for the place; they'd hold week-ly theme nights, fancy dress and the like. One week, they over-reached themselves; it was a Hawaiian Beach Party theme, and the landlord actually bought in a load of real sand which he poured all over the floor. The night was a wash-out, but the sand remained. You know like when you've been at the sea-side, and no matter how careful you've been, when you take your shoes off, you still have to pour loads of sand out of them? Well, it was like that in the Peaks. Years after the Beach Party, the residents of Newton Mills were still waking up on a Saturday morning and thinking 'where have I been?' when they saw the trail of sand which they'd left behind them on their way to bed.

Kev, the landlord, was a star. I don't praise easily, but for him I reserve the highest admiration. And it wasn't just because he served us, rain or shine, pissed or sober, from the age of about fourteen, but because he was a proper character. Stories about what he got up to became a part of local folklore. Like the time he told a disabled lad to fook off out of his pub if he was too pissed to walk properly, or the time he drank four out of the ten bottles on his own top shelf, just because his wife had told him that she thought he should clear up a bit. Going in the Peaks was like going into Kev's front room. As long as you were about as well behaved as him, and made him laugh too, you were alright. He never - apart from the disabled lad - chucked anyone out for making a fool of themselves when drunk. Rather, he'd dish out these yellow cards; one hour 'booze bans', which didn't really mean anything, as you could just get your mates to get you one in anyway.

Anyway, so we wander in the place and it's about as busy as you can expect for a Thursday night. The sweet factory only does a half-day on Fridays so loads of the workers are in, filling their faces with strong lagers. I swear, if you ever buy sweets from that factory, have a check for the 'made on' date. If the sweets were made on a Friday morning, they were most likely made by someone drunker than the tramp you see sitting in his own piss by the station, wherever you live. In fact, don't buy sweets from there at all. The stories I've heard about people wanking into the Dolly Mixture mix, sneezing into the Strawberry Strips or gozzing in the Gobstoppers would be enough to make Willy Wonka turn in his Great Glass Grave.

The sweet factory workers hate anyone who doesn't have to work at their place, and naturally, as we are all fresh-faced individuals, shall we say, they stare us out as soon as that front door swings shut. I'd like to say that silence descended, like in a Saloon Bar in the Wild West, but it doesn't; you can still hear the Rolling Stones screaming 'Sympathy for the Devil' from the same Jukebox that's probably been here since before there was even a pub. If it's not 'Sympathy for the Devil' - to which all the locals quietly sing the 'woo-woo' bits over their stale pints, despite never speaking for the rest of the day - its Christmas songs. Kev thinks it's hilarious to keep ploughing his own money in the machine and playing the full Now Christmas album, from Mudd to Wizzard. He is a bit of a twat that way.

'What can I get you, boys?' asks Kev, non-commitally. He never admits to knowing us in front of the hard-nuts from the sweet factory. He's still sort-of Sheriff of this Toy Town and admitting to knowing us would be like admitting to harbouring criminals, or something.

Key-Ring's surreptitiously counting coppers in his pocket - I know he's doing it. He's waiting for one of us to get the first round in. He's a right tight fooker that one, always malingering behind us, refusing to stick his hand in his pocket. But a bit of a stand off is developing here. Kev has addressed his question directly to Key-Ring, and to back down now would be like suicide.

'D'you not speak English, boy?' snarls Kev.

'I... I need the bog... can one of you get these in?' stumbles Key-Ring, gingerly, oh so very gingerly.

Kev's cruel laughter follows him all the way into the toilets.

'Don't worry lads,' says Kev, leaning over the taps, conspiratorially. His beer belly is trailing in all the drip trays now. 'I'll get the fooker to pay once he's back from having a slash.'

We grin. It's all you can do in here, amongst the meatheads. Toy Town my arse; these guys are more like crack commandos. And you know what I mean by crack.

'Two pints of Miller and a Black Russian,' says Billy. We always drink Miller because for some reason, it's £1.48 in here. It's ace; get back from a night out and you know how many pints you've had by how many 2p coins are in your pocket.

'Black Russian; I ain't ever heard of no Black Russians,' says a bloke to the side of the bar. We hadn't noticed him before; he looks like he's a stone-slab, he's that silently unmoving, so strong, so silent. He's not smiling.

'Err... it gets you pissed,' says Billy, always good in a crisis.

'It's for your mate, ain't it?' asks Stone Slab. 'I'll just go and have a word with him. I've never liked gingers.'

'Don't... we have a gig tonight,' stammers Billy, still doing admirably, in my opinion. I'm not worried though; I've already seen the gleam in Kev's eyes as he pours our pints. This Stony fooker is on a wind-up.

'A gig eh?' he says, and his voice rumbles as though when he moves, the earth's crust moves slightly too.

'Up at the Church Hall,' continues Billy. 'We're just getting a bit of Dutch Courage before we go on.'

'What sort of shit do you play?' asks the Slab, emphasising the word 'shit' as though what we did could never be anything more than excremental.

'Well, we do some of our own stuff, but some covers too. We're doing 'Sound of the Suburbs' tonight...'

''Sound of the Suburbs', Slab almost shouts, 'I fookin love that song.'

'Used to be on the Jukey in here, 'til it got a fook-off scratch on it,' Kev chips in, dropping our pints in front of us. And I mean dropping; most of the foamy contents spill down the sides of the glass and onto the bar.

Key-Ring's back now and in the nick of time. Slab takes him by surprise and claps him on the shoulder, friendly-like. But Key-Ring has no idea about our new musical bond, and instead takes the gesture as one of aggressive intent. He staggers back, away from the Slab. Billy and I share a look of amusement.

Suddenly, Slab starts rumbling - laughing - and then everything is OK again in Toy Town. Key-Ring grins, sheepily, and picks up his Black Russian. He gets his second surprise when Kev asks him for the money for the round. He looks back at us with what looks like genuine fear in his eyes, but finally, he reaches into his coat pocket and pulls out a wallet. I'm sure I see at least three tenners in there before Key-Ring finally clamps it shut.

'What's in a Black Russian then?' asks Key-Ring's new pal.

If there's one thing our Key-Ring knows about then it's booze. I think he reads up on it with the same obsession that other, more normal, fookers devour everything they can about their favourite footballer, or birds with their favourite soaps. He's like a walking boocyclopaedia, the shit he knows. And he can drink it, too. Because he's such a big lad, booze rarely hits the sides. Beer's like pop to him, so way back, he turned to the spirits to get the same kick. Now he's on cocktails, and in the Peaks, a cocktail is about as skilfully made as they are in them bars in Spain. Kev just pours the shit into the glass until it gets to about the right colour - or at least what he can remember is the right colour.

'The original and best Black Russian was a mix of vodka and coffee liqueur,' says Key-Ring, like he's making a documentary. 'It was first made in 1949, in Belgium...'

'You won't find any coffee liqueur in my shit,' interrupts Kev. 'Mine's Vodka and Coke and a bit of rum.'

Key-Ring can't disguise the look of distaste which crosses his gingery-bearded face. Slab looks mildly interested though. 'Make us one then, Kev,' he belches.

Pretty quickly, the Black Russians that our friend the Slab was pouring down his throat with the thirst of a marathon runner, begin to take effect. Where once, his speech had been stonily flat, it's now all over the place. He's had to sit down too, but still, he's downing these drinks at a rate of knots, like he's just discovered that by drinking them, he can add years to his sorry, slabby life. Now don't get me wrong; you know I'd usually drink with anyone, but this cunt is starting to get embarrassing. He's already told Key-Ring that he loves him 'despite being ginger' on three separate occasions now, and I fear that he's going to start trying to sponge off us at any moment. Billy's nervous for other reasons. He keeps nudging me and jerking his head back as though to indicate we should start thinking about walking back to the Church Hall. Fair enough; I've thought about it, can't be bothered yet though.

I'll let Billy and Key-Ring sweat it out. I'm enjoying watching them squirm, especially Key-Ring, who I now realise has clocked that huge goitre on Slab's grey neck, and is starting to feel sick. It's like one of Tunes' spots, only about ten times the size. I watch him start to edge away from the brute across the pew, but his arse is sticking, inconveniently, to the Velcro-like material. He can't get away.

'One more for the road?' I ask.

Suddenly, as I'm leaning over the bar, trying to drag Kev's attention away from this new handheld computer game he's probably bought for his kid but has now claimed for himself, I feel a strong hand clap on my shoulder. Howard is standing there, looking mightily pissed off.

'Don't you think you'd better get your arses up to the Hall?' he asks. 'Look, the Landy's outside; I'll bip you round and you'll be there in five. The evening's going a bit quicker than they anticipated.'

Bip us round, will he? Drive us round the bip? Bipping heck, what the bip's he talking about?

'We're alright, Howard,' I say, but already, I can see the relieved Billy and Key-Ring climbing to their feet, grateful for the reprieve. I could argue some more, but really, I don't see the point. 'Get us a carry-out,' I shout over to Kev, who sighs, signs off his game and pulls a can of Red Stripe from the fridge. I don't bother getting one for either of the Lightweight Brothers.

The Church Hall is a hive of activity; worker-bee cunts bip back and forth, bipping between people, offering their plates full of bipping triangular egg sarnies with their crusts cut off so the old folk can swallow them better. Most people are drinking cups of tea. The lights are startlingly bright after the gloom of the Peaks and wouldn't you know it; it's only now that me head starts spinning a little bit from the ales I've supped.

I walk towards the stage, where I can see Do-Nowt telling-off the mouldy old DJ that's going to be coming on at any second. For me, one amp's as good as another, but Do-Nowt has a sixth sense for these things, and the amp this DJ has brought along is clearly pure shite. Everything seems to be moving in fast forward, like someone's sat their fat arse on the remote. Even Do-Nowt up there seems to be moving with uncharacteristic speed. I feel for the can of Red Stripe in my pocket and it gives me the strength to barrel my way through a varied assortment of old cunts and find the passage-way to the backstage area. There, I crack the can open immediately.

Howard finds me like that, slumped against the wall, pouring the booze down my throat. He grabs me by the shoulders and for a minute I think he's going to shake me, like my dad does - did - sometimes, but he doesn't. I realise he's holding me firmly, but gently, like he's about to whisper something important into my ear. I watch his old, careworn face as he tries to find the right words. I see the pain in his eyes - perhaps it's the reflection of my own eyes. Then he just sighs and takes the can out of my hand. And I let him. I just let him do it.

'Don't ruin it for Billy,' he says finally. And right then, I suddenly don't want to be drunk any more, I want to enable Billy's dad to be proud of him. I want people to be proud of me... I want...

'Girritus back,' I slur, finally realising that I want the can of Red Stripe again.

'You're drunk already,' he says.

'I'm not,' I start arguing, and then realise its useless. There's nothing more obvious a sign of drunkenness than someone having to tell you that they aren't drunk. If you're not smacked out of your head, you don't go about waving your clean arms at people in the streets, do you?

I wander away from Howard and lurch towards Tunes, Billy and Key-Ring who are all huddled around their instruments, strumming little melodies. That trio are like the Holy fookin Trinity; good, do-good, and do-gooder. They look at me as though I'm Satan. Well, they always said that the Devil makes the best music... or was it that he had the best lines? No matter, everyone likes a little bit of evil around.

'What's wrong with you?' asks Tunes as I approach them.

'Nowt,' I say, playing it cool. 'Just getting in the zone.'

'Zoned out, more like,' says Key-Ring. I've said it before

and I'll say it again; the day that fooker says anything remotely funny will be the day I... I, I don't know. But something irreversible will happen, like crossing the streams in Ghostbusters.

While I've been wandering about the hall and having little tête à têtes with Billy's dad, these three have been getting into their togs for the gig. And, I know I can't say much because I'm drunk anyway, but I'm speechless. They look like three fookin lumberjacks on their way back from a hard day's yacker in the trees. They're all wearing these faded check-shirts and denims, topped off by them ridiculous cherry-red Doc Martens that are all the rage amongst shaven-headed lezzers at the moment. It's like they've watched one Nirvana video on MTV and based their whole wardrobes on it. Worse, Tunes has frizzed up his hair so's he can look like Slash out of Guns 'n' Roses, maybe, but really it looks like some polite soul has taken a slash on his head and then moulded it into some uncompromising shapes. Key-Ring's ginger mop is practically glow-in-the-dark, as is his too-pale skin. Billy just looks like Billy, but in fancy dress. And here's me in me stylish black shirt, me trim brown cords and some quality Adidas originals. We look like two different bands - and we probably are.

'Here,' says Billy, handing me something. Ah! The coup de grace; of course; in my semi-drunken state, I'd almost forgotten. And as the DJ starts to play his final track, 'Hi Ho Silver Lining', I'm backstage laughing my young-looking head right off.

Do-Nowt's somehow got a hold of this recording off an old war film from his dad's collection and copied it onto CD or something. I don't know how he did it, but as we enter that dark stage, he's ramming the sound of air raid warnings back down them old cunts' throats. Except, when my eyes get accustomed to the dark, when I look out onto that sea - lake, maybe... OK, pond - of faces, I realise that the older heads have seized the opportunity to scarper. What we're faced with is a crowd made up of the First Year Girls dancing troup, some of the more daring members of the brass band, some of the committee members and the Church Warden.

There's about forty, maybe fifty tops, people in the Church Hall now, and there's not a sign of Tony Wilson and his Granada TV chums. The first wave of disappointment sets in. But fook it, I'm gonna be a professional, so I'm gonna have to know how to deal with difficult crowds. And as the stage lights come on, and they see the get-up we're all in, the crowd starts cheering anyway. Despite myself, I start to feel excited. You see, we've come on wearing gas-masks; Billy's dad found 'em when he cleared out his old man's house after he passed on. We're putting on a show for these motherfookers, brass band goons or not.

And then the first jingly-jangly bars of our version of The Members classic, 'Sound of the Suburbs' kicks in, and we are away. We aren't punks, of course, but the song kind of suits our attitude, and we play a rip-roaring version of it, even if I say so myself. I rip me gas mask off and simply shout the first lines. 'Same old fookin Sunday morning,' I yell with gusto, and realise that I've already broken the no swearing rule. Unconsciously, my eyes scan the crowd. I notice that there's some sort of commotion by the entranceway. Three old men are gesticulating wildly at someone, or something which is trying to get in. They're as animated as they've probably been in about fifty years. Then, like skittles, they are battered apart, and in comes the bowling ball head of Mr. Stony Slab from the Peaks, followed by about twenty of his cronies. They make this mad dash into the middle of the crowd of twelve year old girls just in time for us to launch into the first chorus, and then all hell breaks loose. They turn the gently bipping and bopping crowd into a vicious mosh-pit. Fists are flying everywhere. I'm loving it; I am about sixty percent responsible for this mayhem!

Things are slipping downhill faster than a toboggan with lumpy twat Key-Ring inside. These ageing good-for-nothings have taken over the Church Hall. I can almost hear the teachers asking: 'Is nothing sacred any more?'

Clearly not, because in the gap between our opening cover and one of our own songs, I spy one of Slab's meat-house buddies being shinned up the wall towards the figure of Jesus on his cross which has been attached to the wall. I can see what's going to happen even before it does. Either this clown is going to fall arse over tit and do himself some serious damage, or worse, he's going to do some serious damage to poor old Jesus, who was doing nowt really but hang-out on the wall. I look round at Billy to see if he's seeing what I can see. I notice that Billy's gone to the side of the stage and is in deep conversation with his dad. He's not even sat on his drum stool. I look round at Key-Ring, who's staring at the floor, scared that one of the meaty bastards will come up and kick the crap out of him. Tunes, though, Tunes hasn't noticed a thing. Maybe it's his big hair, although somehow I doubt it. He's lost in the music, man. He starts playing, even when everyone else is staring disaster straight in the face.

Jesus Christ comes down amongst his flock at the precise moment that Billy jumps back behind the drums and smashes into his cymbal. We're off again. Nothing can stop us... and after that day, nothing really could. Of course, the aftermath of the vandalism was pretty bad. We were banned from gigging in most venues in the town, and were given a severe dressing down by the teachers, most of whom hadn't even been bothered to stay anyway, but to be honest, at that point, we knew that we had bigger fish to fry. We'd had our first headline in the local paper: 'The Satanist Sound of the Suburbs', and we knew that we'd never look back.

The article was, of course, a complete character assassination. They even implied that we'd incited the mad meatheads to start pulling the figurine off the wall. Howard wrote an angry letter to the paper, denying all the accusations, and we were kept in the news for the next few weeks by a war of words between him and the Church Warden. It was funny as fook.

Oh, and one more thing before I forget. In the midst of all the mayhem, someone took off with the whole takings from the evening. The extravaganza contributed precisely nothing to the proposed new Sixth Form Block. A certain Danny Nosworthy, Do-Nowt to his friends, suddenly started wearing some expensive-looking threads in the next couple of weeks, however.

Carol Fenlon

Carol Fenlon is a Liverpool/Lancashire lass now living in Skelmersdale where she is close to becoming a disreputable old woman. She is delighted to be allowed to let it all out in Radgepacket again. Read more about her and her published work at www.carolfenlon.com

Half Mile Island

When Julie threw him out, Twodog thought it was the worst day of his life. It hadn't been the best of partnerships but at least he'd had a roof over his head and they'd rubbed along together okay, most of the time, even hit the occasional erotic high.

It wasn't even his fault, it was the dogs that Julie objected to. Rosie developed a penchant for chewing Julie's knickers and Cooper kept getting out and shagging every bitch for miles around so that Julie faced a constant barrage of paternity claims from angry neighbours. Things had come to a head when she'd come home from replacing a drawer full of underwear to find a cardboard box on the doorstep, containing four puppies all with Cooper's unmistakeable mournful eyes.

'It's the last fucking straw.' Julie heaved the box into Twodog's arms, hitting him squarely in the chest. 'Either those dogs go or you do.'

There was no choice really. Rosie and Cooper already had their leads on. Julie had tied them to the leg of the table while she was waiting for Twodog to come back from buying their Saturday lottery tickets. Within half an hour, Twodog was out on the street with his cosy dream of a big win shattered, carrying a backpack with a few clothes and two tins of dogfood, the box of puppies under one arm and Rosie and Cooper straining at the leash on the other. He left the box of puppies outside old Mrs Fairbairn's flat at the bottom of the stairs and went straight to his mum's, but she was on guard as soon as he went in the back door.

'What do you want?'

'Julie threw me out.'

''Bout time that girl got some sense.'

His sister Carmen snickered. They were sitting at the kitchen table drinking coffee and drooling over the latest issue of 'Chat'. Poppy, Carmen's two year old was eating a choc ice under the table.

'You can't stop here.'

'But I've got nowhere to go.'

'You can't bring them dogs here. Think about the baby.'

Poppy let out a wail. The choc ice had vanished down Rosie's throat and Cooper was licking the chocolate from round the baby's mouth.

'See?' Carmen snatched her up and glared at Twodog.

Twodog went round to his mate, Pretty Pe's; so called because he was constantly washing and preening his long, dark hair, although really he was hard as nails.

'Come in.' The crack in the door widened beyond Pe's eye to reveal the rest of him. He hung the axe back on its hook over the lintel as Twodog, Rosie and Cooper bundled inside.

Living with Pretty Pe was worse than living with Julie. The axe was constantly required to calm the druggies in the upstairs flat. Bono, Pretty Pe's staff, regarded the couch where Twodog slept as his own bed and made constant efforts to reclaim it. Cooper fought with Bono and Rosie tried to shag him. There was nothing at all to eat in Pretty Pe's cupboards and fridge, except a bag of dry dog food and a tin of beans. Twodog had to go out and buy milk, coffee, teabags as well as enough food to last the weekend for them both.

On Monday Twodog fell asleep at his desk. His boss gave him a warning. 'You're employed here as security. That means you keep watch, keep the place secure? How do you think it looks to visitors to the plant, you snoring away in the entrance?'

On Thursday, he fell asleep again. This time it was simple. 'Piss off and don't come back.'

He was in Aldi, shopping for dog food when he saw the tents. He'd loved camping as a kid, the freedom, the lack of responsibilities. Yeah, it would be good to get away from it all; Julie, the job, the chaos at Pretty Pe's. As he stood fingering the nylon cover of the tent bag, he knew just the place to go.

Half Mile Island was the biggest roundabout in a town so full of roundabouts that no one who lived there ever noticed them any more. The dense copse in the middle of it afforded the perfect cover. The first night was heaven, the peace and quiet was something Twodog had rarely known. He sat at the edge of the trees, looking up at the stars, the open sky with no hemming houses, no nearby streetlights and contentment crept through his being. Rosie and Cooper were also quiet, as if playing at being wild dogs tweaked something in their own souls.

With his final wages he bought sleeping bags, a gas stove and camping pans. Within a week he was settled in as if he'd always been meant to live like this. He was completely invisible to the outside world, yet could enter it at will. Pretty Pe let him use his address to sign on so he could claim his benefits and to deal with the small necessities of life like the occasional shower and charging his phone. He did his share of job-seeking and kept his head down. Cooper could go off on his amorous adventures without fear of being tracked down and Rosie had plenty of sticks to chew.

The trees protected him from the worst of the rain and it was a warm summer. At night, sitting by his stove, or cosy in his sleeping bag with the dogs cuddled up, Twodog was happy in a way he'd never been with Julie. All in all, it was a pretty good life.

Until the day he found Howard Johnson. 'Course he didn't know who he was when he found him. He didn't know anything in the moment of shock when he saw the body dangling from a big sycamore on the edge of his copse.

'Shit, shit, shit,' was all he could think as the visual information and Rosie's barking flooded his brain, turning it to mush. It was the dog who had summoned him, tugging him from his bed. Cooper had been away for two days on a prolonged courtship somewhere.

Twodog's first instinct was to run but as his shoulder brushed the dangling legs, they kicked slightly and the realization that the man was still alive, focused his thoughts.

'Hello, can you hear me?' Twodog said, desperately running through the first aid procedure he'd learned at his job induction. There was nothing with which to prop up the man's weight so Twodog shinned up the tree fast as he could and fished out his penknife. The branch was solid, the man had made a good choice and the rope, though strong, was made of thin orange nylon stuff, more like string, and Twodog's knife was sharp and made short work of it.

The man crashed to the ground, seemingly unconscious. Twodog climbed down and tried to loosen the knot. The man groaned and lay still again. Twodog felt a slight pulse in his neck. He pulled out his mobile and keyed 999.

Of course it was the end of his idyllic rural life. Although he tried to pretend he had just been passing through, walking his dog, the police had immediately found his tent and he'd been forced to confess.

"HERO LIVED ON HALF MILE ISLAND" the headlines blared in the local paper. Twodog cursed Howard Johnson as he read all about him from his room at the homeless persons' hostel in the town centre. Howard Johnson's wife had left him for another man after he'd lost his job and got into debt. 'Should have got a dog,' Twodog thought bitterly, wondering how Rosie was in the dog pound and whether he would ever see Cooper again.

He almost enjoyed the celebrity though. Johnson sent him a sheepish note of thanks from his hospital bed and the incident was even briefly reported on the six o'clock news. Julie rang and they had a long, tender conversation. Twodog had to admit he'd been a bit lonely on the island, despite the dogs' company and the thought of Julie's warm, round body was tempting. He had to keep reminding himself that after all, she had chucked him out without caring what happened to him.

The next day the nationals got hold of the story. Twodog accepted £500 for an exclusive interview with the Daily Star. 'Cash on the nail, mind,' he stipulated. There was a two page spread in the following day's paper, with a huge picture of himself and Rosie, taken with the permission of the warden at the dog pound. That afternoon a man from the Council came to offer Twodog a flat on the prestigious estate not far from Half Mile Island, a move he could never have aspired to while living with Julie.

'Of course there are no dogs allowed,' the man said, glancing at the open newspaper depicting Twodog and Rosie. Twodog couldn't make up his mind. How could he leave Rosie in the pound, probably to certain death? And what had happened to Cooper? The man gave him forty eight hours to decide, snapped his briefcase shut and departed.

The following morning the hostel staff informed him that a dog answering Cooper's description had been picked up and taken to the pound. They also said that if he didn't accept the Council's housing offer he would have to leave the hostel at the end of the week. What should he choose - security, new home, Julie or freedom, the dogs and another half mile island somewhere? At four o'clock, the hostel manager, Alison, tapped respectfully on his door.

'I've had a phone call from Callie Cross.' she said in awed tones.

Twodog looked blank.

'You know, Callie Cross, the one who does the dog training programme, 'Dreadful Dogs and Beastly Bitches.' She wants to do a TV interview with you. We've set up a meeting for tomorrow afternoon, if it's okay with you.'

Callie Cross was gorgeous, seductive, but horribly bossy. She took Twodog over as if he were a naughty Jack Russell.

'I knew you'd have charisma,' she purred, crossing her legs to give him a glimpse of thigh. 'Anyone who loves dogs as much as you do, has to make a good partner for me. Work partner, I mean,' she gave him a sideways smile. 'I think we could collaborate on a whole series.'

'I can't think straight,' Twodog moaned, putting his head in his hands. 'Everything's happening too fast. My dogs are in the pound, I can't bring them here. I can't have them in my new flat. My girlfriend's trying to railroad me into going back to her but I can't have the dogs there either. I wish I was back on the island, but the police won't let me go back there. I don't know what to do. It's all that Howard Johnson's fault. I wish I'd just left him there.'

'Bring them out to my kennels,' Callie Cross said. 'You can come and work for me, there's a rent free cottage, it's out in the country, you'll love it.'

Twodog was tempted but he knew in his heart what she wanted. She was the kind of woman who had to control everyone she met. She would tame him, make him her pet. He would end up a puppy on a string, barking.

'I'll have to think about it,' he said, just to get rid of her so he could get his head straight.

She shrugged her shoulders, making her breasts wobble in her low cut tee shirt. 'I'll send a car for you tomorrow at two.'

Twodog tossed and turned all night but by the morning he'd come to a decision. He drew out the £500 he'd got from the Star and paid the bounties on Rosie and Cooper. There was a lot of barking and licking, tail wagging and wriggling before he could get their leads on and take them away.

'I'm leaving,' he said to an astonished Alison as he marched both dogs into the hostel. He packed his tent and camping gear. It was amazing how few possessions he really needed.

As he set off down the road a smooth black Saab passed him and pulled up outside the hostel. The driver wore a peaked cap. Callie Cross was in the passenger seat. Twodog kept walking. Somewhere there was another Half Mile Island waiting for the three of them, a free place where a man and his dogs could look up at the moon and the stars.

On the other hand winter was coming. Soon it would be bloody freezing. Twodog turned back to the big car. Callie Cross opened the back door and the three of them jumped in.

<u>Danny King</u>

Danny is the author of nine books, the latest being *'More Burglar Diaries'* (published by Byker Books...as if you didn't know).

Before this he worked for top literary tome/naughty bongo mag, Club International, where an earlier version of this story first appeared. It is republished here with big thanks to Rob Swift.

It Started With A Diss

For some people, school days were the best days of their lives. For others they were a continuous series of humiliating slaps around the chops. I know it's not possible, but when I think back to my final years at school, I can remember doing nothing else other than crawling around on all fours after my glasses while everyone kicked me up the arse, much to the amusement of every girl I ever cared for.

That said no two words make me groan louder than the name Julie Mason. She was my obsession, my distraction and the reason I left school at the earliest opportunity with no qualifications.

I will explain.

From the very first time I laid eyes on Julie, I knew she was 'the one'. Unfortunately, when she first saw me, I think she just thought I was 'the two'.

She was thirteen and so was I.

She was in Mr Tanner's Art class and so was I.

She was beautiful, smart and popular. Did I already mention I was in Mr Tanner's Art class as well?

God I fancied her like mad. No actually, that's not right. Fancied her? That makes it sound so grubby. So base. My affections for Julie were more than that. They were higher. Purer. I loved Julie Mason. That's it; I loved her.

And I celebrated this love by smashing myself to sleep every night thinking about her.

The trouble was I was painfully shy. She only needed to look at me and I would burn up, at which point someone would always helpfully point out: 'Hey look everyone, Joe 90's gone red!'

On the odd occasion I actually spoke to her, I would lose it completely. Example: She would say something to me like: 'You're in 2NN aren't you? Give Emma Philips a message from me. Tell her to meet me at the gates at one o'clock.'

To which I would reply: 'I'm not Emma, I'm Danny,' followed by a bright red glow-on.

I was thirteen. I fancied a girl. The rules were simple. I had to avoid her at all costs. I had to sit as far away from her in class as I could. And I had to diss her whenever her name was mentioned. In short, I had to do everything I could to convince her and the rest of the civilised world that I hated Julie Mason and everything she stood for. The consequences of anyone finding out any different were far too dire to consider. Life, as I knew it, would be over.

Very, very occasionally, someone would take a guess and say: 'You fancy Julie, don't you?'

And without thinking, I'd have to quickly reply: 'No I don't, I think she stinks like a bucket of piss.'

One time, this didn't do enough to dissuade my accuser and he squealed with delight: 'Yes you do, you fancy Julie Mason. Hoohooo hohohohoooh!'

Of course, with hindsight, the answer I should've given was this: 'Yeah? So what?'

To which his only possible response would've been: 'Hoohooo hohohohoooh!' But I was thirteen and full of self-doubt. Only Morrissey understood.

There were just two ways I was permitted to express my feelings for a girl in those days; I could either repeatedly bomb past her house on my bike. Or, come the start of the third year, I could find out what options she was taking and sign up for all the same classes in order to get to know (or as it's come to be known, stalk) her.

So this is what I did.

It's also the reason I came to leave school without a single qualification. See while I was good at Woodwork, Metalwork, Geography and Art, Julie wasn't, so I ended up taking History, Drama, Home Economics and RE.

Saying that though, Drama did provide numerous opportunities to make contact with her, most notably during the school play when I was playing second 'man' and she was one of the make-up girls. How I adored having her apply the greasepaint. How I would smudge her work the first chance I got in order to go back for a retouch. And how I nearly died when during one such application Julie noticed I was floating a pocket battleship in my leotard and refused to go near me again.

Over the next year or so though, I got to know her on a name-calling basis; I'd refer to her as fatty, spotty, goofy or anything else I could think of in order to provoke a reaction out of her and she would call me maggot, wanker and so on. It was hardly Romeo and Juliet but at least we were talking.

We ticked along like this for a while and the antagonism was just starting to turn into affection when things took a turn for the nasty. Graham Benton had thrown a party at his house one Saturday night (obviously I found out about this the following Monday morning) and, according to the rumours, had fingered Julie in his back garden after she'd got drunk. We found out some months later that this wasn't true, that actually Graham had spread this lie in order to get back at her after she'd got off with him but had refused to let things get beyond a tit-up. Julie had been sweet on Graham for ages and was therefore distraught by this betrayal. But like I said, none of us knew any of this at the time. We all believed the lie.

I was devastated.

I didn't talk to anyone for several days and avoided Julie like the plague. Though when I finally did bump into her and her mates near the History block, I doubt I could've made things worse had I picked up a handful of dog shit, yanked open her collar and shoved it down her back.

'Hello Joe 90,' she smiled, 'had any boners lately?'

'Fuck off slag and go and get fingered again!' I snarled.

Julie and her little entourage just stared at me without saying a word before finally turning and walking away like ghosts, making me wonder if I might've gone a tad too far with that one. I gave it a couple of days in the hope that everyone would forget about my little witticism before approaching Julie again, though I didn't get more than half a word out before her friend Emma turned and screamed at me: 'JUST PISS OFF AND LEAVE HER ALONE!!!!' with a level of hatred that only teenage girls can muster.

That hatred lingered for three more years, right up to, and through, our O-levels.

I lasted only two and a half.

Bugger.

Ian Ayris

Ian hears voices. Sweary, naughty voices. Telling him tales of silly things and random acts of violence. Instead of seeking psychiatric help, he writes these stories down and sends them to Byker Books. Surviving on Pot Noodles and delusions, Ian awaits sectioning by the authorities, aware that his lifelong support of Dagenham & Redbridge merely strengthens the case against him.

Little Otis

Otis spit sideways, wiped his mouth, and chased after me with an empty can of Fosters in his hand. Little bleeder's only seven but he's mad as they fuckin' come. Whole fuckin' family's mental. Take the old man - Psycho Sol. The Old Bill did. Five years back. Give him a seven stretch for settin' fire to the neighbour's dog. Kept shittin' on his lawn, so one day, when it's doin' it's business, Sol creeps up and takes his lighter to it and . . . WOOF.

Tried lightin' up the Old Bill when they come an' all, standin' there flashin' his lighter like it's some sort of fuckin' flamethrower. The Old Bill's just pissin' 'emselves. Waited for the lighter to go out, then jumped the cunt.

Sols' got five kids, all with his old girl - Shirelle. She used to be Doreen, but Sol made her change her name. Mad on music, Sol, see. Loved the old Atlantic Soul stuff from the sixties. That's how Otis got his name - Otis Redding. And the others. Mind you, they weren't so lucky. Especially Aretha. He had a right fuckin' time of it at school. Poor bastard ended up goin' to some fancy art college down in Brighton just to get away. Saw him when I was down there with the lads last year. He was doin' some drag act on the pier with a little dog called Puff and he was all dressed in some pink leotard bollocks. I think if Sol had been there, he'd have jumped up on that stage and ripped his fuckin' arms right off. Mind you, he weren't very good.

The other three, the twins Percy Sledge and Booker T, and Rufus Thomas, they're still at home, like Otis. Percy and Booker, they're ten, and Rufus has nearly left school, so he's gotta be fifteen or something. Not that he's ever at school. Always hangin' about outside my house, sittin' on the wall, suckin' on a spliff.

He's all right, Rufus. Just the puff's really fucked him up. Paranoid, you know. I've only gotta open the front door and he's runnin' down the street. Either that or he jumps off the front wall and crouches down behind it, hiding like. 'Cept it's always the wrong side, you know, in the garden. Best ignore him. That's what I normally do. Walk down the path pretendin' I don't see him, then off down the street, shakin' me head. Sometimes I look round, and he's back on the wall, but soon as he sees me, he's back off again, this time hidin' on the street side. Look back three or four times, sometimes, when I'm bored. Just to see him fallin' off the wall.

So I got Otis chasin' me with this beer can in his hand. I'm nearly forty and I ain't as fit as I used to be. He's put a spurt on, and the fucker's catchin' up. I can see Shirelle at the door shakin' her fist at me.

'Fuckin' get him, Otis,' she yells. 'Fuckin' have him.'

Like I said. Proper scum.

I'm near the end of the street, just about turnin' the corner. Get out of sight of the little sod and I'll be all right. He'll give up then. But I'm strugglin'. Slowin' down. Can't go on. Do anything to neck the can of Falstaff I nicked off him, but I ain't got the time.

I'm fucked, sittin' on the pavement, back against the passenger door of a light blue Cortina.

Here he is. Otis Redding.

He's starin' at me with them evil little eyes, and his face is red, like a tomato. Chucks the empty beer can at me head, and digs in his pocket.

Pulls out a lighter.

Fuck.

Steve Porter

Steve was born in Inverness and also spent ten years in radge Edinburgh before moving to Spain in 1998. He has recently finished a fictional memoir combining his Moray Firth childhood with his translator alter ego. He's also published poetry, a travel memoir (Iberian Horseshoe) and short stories at Laura Hird, Dogmatika, Parasitic and Glasgow Review.

Blurred Girl Diaries

5 March

My job isn't great but the girl on the bus makes the journey interesting. Neat black business suit, stilettos and shiny dark nylons showing at the ankle. She taps a text message into her mobile phone. Five minutes pass and then she gets off. Tall and slim with equine teeth. Mice End seems like the wrong destination for her.

6 March

There she goes again. All in black: ankle boots with high heels, pencil skirt, opaque tights, handbag and jacket. I take a seat near the back and study her profile. She stands halfway down the bus on the left, listening to music on head-phones. Pop standards most likely. Nothing too weird. I bet she's a funny one in bed though.

8 March

At lunchtime, some guy from the factory gives me a lift to my usual stop. We discuss the merits of Nebraska. Then I get out and shelter in the doorway of a Mice End high rise. A few spits of rain fall on my copy of Brave New World. It's been threatening to rain all morning.

As she climbs the steps, I get an eyeful of her brown tan patterned fishnets and pointed stilettos with straps above the ankles. Is this a basic instinct I'm feeling or something more emotional that the brave new world would frown upon? I'm right behind her as we board the bus. Her thighs are hidden under a stylish black raincoat and a black mini-skirt. She stands in her usual place on the short journey, her coat partly unbuttoned, showing off those long bird-like legs. Imagine working in an office next to that. Below the raincoat, a lime green top covers her modest tits. She knows that her legs are her best assets. I can't help wondering if this is all for my benefit. She must have noticed by now that I like to take up a position where I can watch her.

She puts on her headphones and listens to music, occasionally casting furtive glances backwards. Despite the leggy distraction, I take note of the large silver earrings and wonder if she has dyed her hair. It's a deeper, shinier black. I get off at my usual stop. My cock feels like a revolver that could go off at any minute. It's a very uncomfortable fifteen minute walk home. My pants are wet with pre-cum and my briefcase barely touches the floor before I toss myself off as violently as a fourteen-year-old.

9 March

I'm dating the girl on the bus. We're talking, laughing together, nodding in agreement. She reaches out and touches my hand. Seconds later, the alarm clock rings and I wake up. I want to have this dream every night for the next forty years. That's all it will ever be. She is probably married or at least has a live-in boyfriend. It's Saturday today. I hate sport and mediocre movies. There's nothing to do but think about all this.

20 March

It's been a while. My shifts at the Mice End factory don't coincide with her lunchtime visits home. She gets on the bus and stops at the front for a moment. The driver brakes suddenly. One or two passengers who haven't sat down skate forward. She's holding onto a rail while talking on the telephone. I'm too far back to hear a word she says. Her telephone bills must be sky-high. I wouldn't mind paying them. Perhaps they would be lower as she could talk to me instead. She soon moves to her usual spot. Her clothes are casual and unremarkable. I like the brown jacket though. It hugs her body and compliments her fine slender waist. She's wearing jeans and brown desert boots. She has several pairs of glasses. Today's pair have transparent frames and appear a little

old-fashioned. This look is not far removed from that of the
typical female Mice Ender, minus the flab. Her hair is getting
longer and is dishevelled. It's what the tabloids call 'a just out
of bed look'. Perhaps that's the case and her boyfriend has
just sorted her out. Maybe she's so thin because she spends
her lunch hour losing rather than gaining calories. She ends
the phone call, opens a blue folder and starts flicking through
pages of notes. She could be a student or a teacher. There's
no more time to speculate. I've arrived at my stop.

24 March

Beige leather jacket with an untied belt hanging from the
svelte waist, beige kitten heels, a beige handbag and even a
beige purse, which she opens. I'm sitting just behind her this
time but don't manage to get a glance at her ID cards. Only
blue jeans interrupt the colour scheme and her hair is ruffled
again. I like the combination. Beige is the new black.
Occasionally she turns round and we almost exchange
glances. I'm reading a book called The Invention of Solitude.
The title doesn't make much sense. Nobody invented solitude. It's just there, like shit happens.

25 March

We meet twice today. I'm surprised to see her when I get on
the bus to the factory. This hasn't happened since our first
encounter. She's normally one bus ahead on the way to Mice
End. We look at each other and smile but neither of us say
hello. She's dressed in black. Even a guy, almost blind to
these matters, cannot help but notice colour-coordination is
a big issue with her. The beige handbag has been substituted
for a large black one. She's wearing a knee-length coat,
dress, patterned tights (or stockings?) with stiletto pumps.
All black. In short, an impressive look. When she dresses like
this it makes her hair look darker, newly dyed, but maybe it's
all part of an illusion she creates. Later, we get on at the
same stop to return to the city. Nothing much has changed,

118

except her hair is a mess. It's a cold, windy day in Mice End, so that could explain it. Anyway, I've come to the conclusion she has a boyfriend rather than a husband. They lose interest after marriage, don't they? I wonder if she looks this horny when she gets up in the morning.

28 March

It's a black week. Black dress, black raincoat, black skirt, sheer black tights, buckled stilettos and black skies, which keep her at home. I don't see her at all but I think of these things.

5 April

During her absences I notice other commuters. Young women I see more often than the blurred girl. In fact, there's one I see on my bus to Mice End every day without fail. A cracker she is too; in a predictable sort of way. Mid-twenties, long blonde pony tail. Skin tight jeans with big white boots or white stilettos. I can see a tattoo on the top of her foot if it's a warm, dry day. There's another blonde as well with long black boots and great make up. The blusher on her face makes it look as if she's having a constant orgasm. She's class actually. But out of my league.

8 April

The spring look. The beige outfit with jeans. Quite stylish. Fine in a catalogue but not the biggest turn on. I haven't paid that much attention to her arse before but it does fit nicely into those denims. Skinny legs; meatier in the right places. She drops her bus pass on the floor and doesn't notice. My stop is next so it would be perfectly natural to get up, hand it back to her, receive approval and maybe even get a conversation going. By the time I've run through the possibilities in my mind and risen from my seat, the girl with the tattoo on her foot has picked it up for her. The blurred girl is listening to music. She nods appreciatively and smiles like a mare. I exit stage right without being seen.

13 April

No girl.

2 May

Why didn't I pick up that bus pass?

16 June

Still no sign of her. She could have finished her college course. Maybe she's pregnant. She might even be dead.

17 June

I assume the worst. I heard about a car crash that killed a young Mice End couple recently. This would explain her long absence. I decide to think about her less and focus on working harder now I've become a Human Resources Manager.

30 June

This is my first day in the company car. I don't have to take the bus any more. Due to my improved financial position, I will have new lifestyle choices.

2 September

It's been a busy week. On the way home, I pull into one of those places off the motorway. Girls hang about with guys at the bar. They all come and go. I have a brandy. Then I go to piss it out and return to the bar for another. I light a cigar and wait to be approached. A blonde eventually comes up and makes some idle chat. I don't hear her. I think about making my excuses but remember that I'm not there for the conversation anyway. She might be able to show me a thing or two.

Another girl enters. Black pencil skirt, mega mesh fishnet tights, buckled stilettos, lime top, no raincoat. We are face to face.

'Haven't we met before?' she asks, in an accent that isn't local but has faint traces of Mice End.

'Indeed we have.'

'Shall we?' She takes my hand and hints towards the rooms above us with her brown eyes.

'Why not?'

She leads me out. On the way upstairs, I take a closer look at the network that links her legs to the world.

We enter Room 101.

'Would you like another drink?' she asks. 'Or shall we just get down to it?'

There are numerous possibilities for conversation. The bus route. Text messaging and phone bills. The blue folder. Clothes shops. Whether she has a boyfriend, and if so, does he know what she's now doing for a living? And how the hell did it come to that? But instead I keep things strictly professional and hand over the money.

'We've wasted enough time,' I say. 'Let's see if you live up to expectations.'

Callum Mitchell

Due to an unhealthy obsession with James Bond as a kid, Callum always dreamed of becoming a spy in later life. However, having watched that dream disintegrate before his eyes, he turned to writing; his work has appeared in many publications as well as performances at festivals. He hates Chris Moyles **(*Good Lad-Ed!*)** Read more at: http://callummitchell.co.uk

Broken Hearts and Broken Glass

Coming up on pills while coming up the stairs, Daz feels like an angel floating upon fluffy mushroom clouds up in Heaven. They're a bit fucking spicy. Just dropping one is easily enough to get you shitfaced and climbing the walls like some kind of gurning Spiderman... but Daz didn't settle on just one. No way, Jose. He's on a mission tonight, is Daz. A mission to get proper fucked. Completely cunted. Poor Daz doesn't wanna feel anything but love and some false sense of happiness for the next couple of hours. He's put up with enough shit and heartbreak for one day.

Just a couple of hours ago, Daz was sitting at home in his bedroom with his curtains drawn as he whacked off to some porno his best mate Jay had leant him. It was German. Or Austrian, perhaps. Daz wasn't entirely sure, but it was good stuff all the same. He was just about to blow his load when he heard his Mum bellow up from below.

'Daz - come down here please, love.'

Cursing his old dear for spoiling his fun, Daz went soft instantly, before throwing on his trackie bottoms and making his way down to the front room, where his Mum had Loose Women squeaking out the box. Daz's mum, Shirley, had just got back from the doctors and had this concerned look spread across her pale chops which he hadn't seen in some time. In fact, the last time Daz could remember seeing that look was when he banged his head falling off his bike as a nipper, and blood had pissed from his skull as Shirley screamed and frantically rushed him up to the hospital. Daz could tell something was wrong, he knew his Mum too well. He sat down on the arm of their knackered old burgundy sofa and tried his hardest not to burst into tears as Shirley told him she had been diagnosed with lung cancer. Just as she finished telling him, she leant forward, reached into her handbag and withdrew a Richmond Superking, which she then asked Daz to light for her. Still in complete shock, he lit his Mum's ciggie and then took one for himself. He didn't know what to say. Why would he? This was all completely new and surreal to our Daz. If he had a dad, perhaps he could talk to him about it. Or even if he had a brother, or sister, or something. But it's just Daz and Shirley. No one else. And now Daz was being told that soon he wouldn't have Shirley either. How fucking cruel is that?

He reaches the top of the stairs in The Club; feeling the love, feeling the rush. Jay follows close behind; he's trying his hardest to give Daz a good night out after the day he's just had. That's why he's fed him three little fellas already, and that's why he reckons it'd be a good idea to get a round of Sambucas in. Quench the thirst, soothe the pain. He's a good mate, is Jay.

*****

Carly is loitering by the bar. She's feeling a bit guilty tonight as she stands there looking all sexy with make up splurged across her face, and her bouncy boobs climbing out of her dress. Carly is feeling guilty because last night she cheated on her boyfriend, Keith, with his best mate, Mikey. She never meant to. It just kind of happened.

They were getting mashed around Keith's flat; Carly, Keith, Mikey, Jason and Bex. The boys were on beer, while the girls glugged vinegary vino by the bottle. Keith makes a living from shifting pills and MaDMAn, and decided to dish a few freebies out to everyone. Nobody declined, instead scoffing their faces with the free drugs like they were penny sweets. It wasn't long before everybody was fucked. Keith never knows when to stop, so he kept shoving more and more MaDMAn into his gob, whilst everyone else was content as they were. Jason and Bex started getting frisky in the corner, their tongues twisting in their mouths, and their hands finding each other's naughty bits. Before long, they were practically fucking right in front of everyone. Carly, Mikey and Keith watched on hysterically, eating more drugs and drinking more booze.

Eventually, Jason and Bex announced that they were leaving, disappearing into the night and off for a euphoric shag.

That left Mikey, Keith and Carly, all huddled together, gurning their tits off...well, Carly was the only one with actual tits, but you get the picture. Anyway, Keith was so off his rocker that he soon passed out, and began snoring loudly through his Mud-blocked nostrils. Carly and Mikey chatted for a while, and both of them were feeling all loved up and horny, when Carly said it was about time she went to bed. She tried waking Keith but he didn't budge, so she clambered to her feet, said goodnight to Mikey with a big grin, pecked him on the cheek, and wandered into Keith's bedroom. She hadn't even shut the door, when Mikey came charging in behind, passionately snogging her - tongue and all - as they fell onto the bed. They sucked and stroked and fucked and poked. Both of them, like caged animals being released, they tore their clothes off and didn't stop to think about Keith for a moment. Carly rode him like a racehorse, and can't even remember if she made him wear a Johnny or not. She was certain of one thing though, Keith had never given her an orgasm like that! Mikey scarpered home almost as soon as he had come, which was probably a good thing really, although Carly couldn't sleep a wink all night and kept fantasising over a rematch. At some point, hours later, Keith crawled into bed and tried getting a little friendly, but Carly just pretended she was snoozing.

She's been feeling bad about it all day. Part of her is wishing she and Mikey were an item, so that she could just 'fess up' to everything that happened last night. He's better looking than Keith, and definitely a better shag; but despite Keith being a lowlife drug-dealer and moron, he has always looked after Carly, and Christ knows what he would do if he found out she had fucked his best mate.

So for now, Carly stands at the bar being perved on by all sorts of greasy rugger lads, as Keith chats away to Mikey - who keeps throwing Carly these filthy smiles which make her go weak at the knees - none the wiser that the two of them bumped uglies in the early hours of this morning. Carly stands there, sipping her Smirnoff Ice and waiting for the bomb of MaDMAn Keith gave her to kick in.

The dance floor is heaving with a swarm of sweaty, writhing bodies all gyrating their hips, wiggling their bums and shaking what their mammies' gave em. There are desperate single mums searching for paralytic young hunks to take home and bonk; gorgeous girls unaware that various beef-cakes have spiked their drinks and are planning to drag them out back as soon as no-one's watching; gurning gay boys dressed in pink polo shirts and salivating at the mouths; creepy old pervs drooling over anything with a pair of tits; and hippies smelling of bonfires and tweaking out on mushrooms, but ultimately loving life all the same. The DJ slowly fades in the next record and the crowd start going wild, as boys and girls pair up, and grope and grind on each other with really serious expressions on their face. People throw shapes like a shot-putter on speed. Oh, to be a sober person looking in at this sight. If only. But the problem is, there isn't one sober person here. Everyone is completely off their fucking box. The punters, the bar staff, the bouncers...or at least that's how it seems, anyway. Everyone is having the time of their life, and everyone is doing the Macarena. Hey, Macarena.

***

Meanwhile, Oscar waits at the other end of the bar, scouring The Club for talent. Just along from him is Carly, who Oscar would definitely love to fuck, but she goes out with Keith, who's a complete fucking idiot but also completely fucking mental. And Oscar ain't gonna risk getting on the wrong side of that horrible cunt. No chance. He scans the room and spies with his little eye, a flock of flirtatious females fixing for a fuck. There are six of them huddled in the corner like witches round a cauldron. SJ, Tammie, Alice, Becky, Sally and Jade. Oscar eyes each one of them up, weighing out their pros and cons and thinking which one he'd most like to stick his sausage between tonight. He's had four of the six before. SJ, Alice, Becky and Sally. That leaves Tammie and Jade. Tammie is the least attractive of the bunch, with her frumpy figure and spotty chops, so it's got to be Jade then. He orders another drink from the barmaid - Suzie, Oscar's fucked her too - and as he waits for his Jack Daniels and Coke, Oscar tries to catch the eye of Jade. She's not a goddess by any means, but she's definitely worth a squirt. Blonde hair, blue eyes, tidy body... Hitler would have loved Jade.

Suzie serves Oscar his drink; he pays, takes a swig and decides it's time he got his game on. He slyly sniffs his armpits: Lynx Java, nice. Checks his hair in the reflection of the glass: big quiff, Brylcreem does the trick. He takes another gulp of the black stuff and is just about to walk on over Danny Zucco-style, when the sound of glass smashing and sudden pandemonium breaking out forces him to have a goosey gander at what's occurring.

***

So Carly decided to tell Keith about her and Mikey. Once again, she didn't mean to. She never means to fuck up does Carly. What happened was...

She was down in the toilets taking a leak and chatting to her mate Hollz, who isn't really her mate, as Carly thinks she's a bitch most of the time, but still when you're bladdered you do and say all sorts of things that you wouldn't normally do. They had both just finished pissing in their respective cubicles, when Carly felt the MaDMAn kick in and was suddenly all wobbly and woozy. Hollz started chatting to her and asking if she was okay, but everything she said was s...l...o...w...a...n...d...s...l...u...r...r...e...d... and all Carly could think about was how much she loved Keith, and how badly she had wronged him by banging his best mate. Without really knowing what she was saying, she began spilling her heart out to Hollz - just about managing not to spill her guts up in the bog at the same time - and told her what she had done. She asked what Hollz thought she should do about it, and Hollz declared that it's always best to be truthful in these situations. Feeling enlightened, Carly agreed, told Hollz she loved her and she was her best mate - although that would change tomorrow morning, fucking slag - and staggered back into The Club in search of Keith.

***

Keith was chatting bullshit to Mikey about how he was always giving Carly multiple orgasms whenever they had sex, when Carly tapped him on the shoulder and announced that they needed to talk. Mikey suddenly got all nervous and edgy, as Carly blurted out what had happened between the pair of them the night before. For a minute it looked like he might try and scarper, but he delayed it that split second too long, and Keith - now in a fit of rage, red mist hovering in front of his eyes - smashed his glass on the edge of the bar, and then jabbed a jagged edge of one of the remaining shards into Mikey's handsome little face. Screams and shouting filled the air, as a stream of crimson shot from Mikey's chops and he sank to the floor, howling in agony. Keith wasn't intent with letting him off that easy though, and before any-one could stop him, he brought his Reebok Classics down on Mikey's head... over and over like a monkey with a miniature cymbal, just to make sure the glass was properly embedded in the lying cunt's flesh. Other people started getting involved, but Keith didn't care. He swung his fists and kicked out his legs, not giving two shits about who he struck along the way. He was furious now. Raging fucking bullfrog. Mikey jerked beneath him like he was having some kind of fit, and then Keith felt the hands of the Four Burly Bastard Bouncers grappling with him and trying to get him on the floor. He landed a punch on one of their noses, but they soon had a grip, and dragged him out the far fire escape where three of them proceeded to give Keith a proper good stamping, with Carly being held back by the other Burly Bastard Bouncer, who was having a good grope and telling her to shut her gob. Fourteen stomps later, Keith eventually stopped moving and the four Burly Bastard Bouncers waited for the pigs to arrive as Carly sobbed hysterically into her tits. What a night!

***

Just around the corner, Daz had managed to get lucky with a girl called Jade - blonde hair, blue eyes, tidy body, maybe you know her? And they were going at it like rabbits in the alleyway that ran parallel to The Club. All in all, Daz had ended up having a top night considering how shit his day had been. As he gave a few final thrusts into Jade though, he was a little bit concerned by all the crying and screaming going on around the corner.

Guy Mankowski

Guy was brought up on the Isle of Wight, but after becoming bored of being the youngest person in a thirty mile radius he moved to Newcastle upon Tyne. Along the way he has struggled as a musician, assistant psychologist and most recently as a writer. His first novella was published by Legend Press in April 2009.

Queens Of The Guestlist

Everyone knows the moment The Queens of The Guestlist have arrived. Until then the evening has somehow seemed contained; though the city lights outside contain promise nothing about them burns furiously until they appear. Disenchanted youths sprawl around bar stools, supping on diluted vodkas, but that changes when the doors to 'The Star and Garter' are swept open as The Queens trip inside. They're a riot of fake fur and plastic pearls, of sugared lips and wide painted eyes. Ruby's wearing a dazzling blue dress and a fake fox-skin stole, her heavy black fringe shining as bright as her pink candy floss lips. Colette clutches a gold handbag that shimmers in perfect synchronicity with her platinum heels, her long snow-white body sparking a scarlet dress to life. She sweeps her cropped blonde fringe to one side and looks up through frosted Edie Sedgwick eyelashes. On arrival both of them bring a powerful aura of lust to the Newcastle bar, a sortilege of perfume and girlish sweat that intoxicates all the nearby men. The Queens are a two-headed sexual predator in tottering heels, clicking their fingers at some stranger on the other side of the bar who may not have even seen them, giggling at some joke beyond the comprehension of mere mortals. This is how their night always begins, and this illusory sense of control is all too important to these faux-exotic creatures.

Colette stands proudly at the bar, burrowing through her sequin handbag for a fiver we all know she will never find. The owner of the bar (Gary, thirty two, haircut of a fourteen year old) is caught by her flash of a smile and drawn over.

'Good evening Missy,' he says, looking as absent-minded as he can, but secretly hoping his girlfriend won't return from her cigarette run soon.

'A'll have a double vodka and soda water- touch of lime please Gary - as soon as I can find me note,' Colette flutters, while Ruby's eyes flick over her shoulders at the men by the jukebox.

132

Gary looks away, feigning boredom. 'It's alreet Collette these are on me, divn't ye fret- though make sure you take another batch of fliers with youse to the club.'

Colette pulls her painted fingers from her handbag with an incredulous look of mock-surprise. 'Gary, you're a star!' she reaches over the bar and kisses him squarely on the cheek, leaving a perfect lipstick mark there for everyone to see. Their pact is complete.

'Ruby will have a double gin and tonic an' all, touch of lime - won't you sugar?'

'Aye,' Ruby says, barely acknowledging Gary as he hoses off a couple of drinks he can't afford to give away.

She pulls closer to Colette and flicks her eyes around the room.

'Who you after?' Colette whispers conspiratorially.

'The Irish boy from the other night, I think his mates are out.' she replies before checking her archaic phone, and then stuffing it away guiltily.

'Let me wear that hairclip.' she begs Colette.

Colette suddenly looks serious. She's spent an hour coiffing her hair with toxic hairspray, just to achieve that stiff Cyndi Lauper look, and she's not going to let Ruby tumble the edifice just so she can get laid.

'I can't get it out now, not here,' Collette says urgently. 'It's in too deep.'

Ruby undergoes a quick sequence of events that will become compulsive as the evening wears on. In a streak of scarlet fingernails she pulls a tiny compact from her handbag, opens it quickly above her head, pouts hard into it, fluffs the hair at the back of her head, checks her fringe, and then closes it in a flash. She sips her drink, careful not to rub off her lip-gloss.

'Lend us a tab Coll, I'm dying. I need a hit of menthol to calm me nerves.' she pleads.

The back door flaps open - not the front door Colette and Ruby flounced through, but the tradesmen's entrance. Like a multi-boobed animal with too many legs, another two girls pour in from the northern night and shimmy towards the bar.

'What the Christ is Roz wearing?' Colette stage-whispers as they meet their eye.

Roz's busty body is pressed into an emerald dress and her sea green stilettos are sparkling like cheap sex under the light of the optics.

'She looks like a Brazilian rainforest.' Ruby whispers, streaking on another layer of glitter from nowhere.

'Girls girls girls!' Collette calls, like an heiress running a garden party, as the two fringes come over.

'You both look gorgeous, youse are so gonna end up pregnant the neet.' she declares. They air kiss each other. Gary rolls his eyes, as he knows he'll soon be handing over even more free cocktails.

The youngest fringe, a brunette who's slightly overdone the leopard print, orders a taxi to the nightclub.

'Get one of those ones where it's just a man pedalling!' Ruby says.

She prefers to ride to the club by rickshaw than a taxi. It's easier to throw coins at the driver and avoid proper payment than with a real taxi, and they have the added bonus of causing a scene when they pull up outside.

Having adjusted their tiaras, in two minutes the girls are all pressed into a rickshaw, having persuaded the young driver to let four of them on. He looks like he's about to have a cardiac arrest, but is desperate for them not to notice. The girls queuing outside the nightclub scowl as they pull up beside them. The Queens are in the grip of some hysterical joke with the driver, who does look like he's about to die.

'Oi Colette, give us a tug!' one of the boys in the queue yells.

'I haven't got time to find it the neet,' she shouts back, not missing a beat.

'Cheeky shite.' Ruby whispers, checking her phone to see if the Irish boy has texted yet.

'Quite fit though,' Colette replies, 'but have you seen his bird? She looks like Lily Allen with Aids.'

'Good evening girls,' the bouncer booms, his face threatening an expression for the first time that day.

'Looking good the neet mind,' he growls as they pass. Colette makes sure she pinches his bicep at the precise moment three of the fringes file behind him, so they don't have to pay.

'You been working out Terry?' she asks, cocking her head to one side.

'Get inside before you get yerself in trouble with us.' Terry replies. He and the other bouncer focus on their tiny arses as they dance towards the cloakroom.

The girls shed their fur at the cloakroom, Colette checking her cheekbones in the hallway mirror. They kick through the double doors to the dance floor; the club is already near full. Miss Newcastle 2009 shimmies past them in a black one piece from Karen Millen.

'Slut.' they all chorus, quietly.

As she draws near her Colette whispers 'Hello babe,' while simultaneously taking out the fliers Gary gave her and pinning them under a nearby pint glass. The two girls air kiss, hold the tips of each other's fingers and then part, all smiles. As she moves away, Colette murmurs 'She looks like she's just had a Christmas dinner'.

They stride purposefully to the dance floor, like a glitter-drenched legion of spandex soldiers, moving onto a battlefield of almost-broken hearts. The DJ notes their arrival, and puts on Bowie's 'Fame' in tribute.

As if it's been agreed without words, The Queens throw their handbags onto the dance floor and step into a circle. With their chins held high and their hands above their heads, they look as if they're wading through treacle. The girls dance slowly, careful not to perspire. As the song fades they move like a nylon tribe to the bar. The girls erupt into shrieks at the sight of a shy looking boy with a messy fringe, carrying a stack of vinyl under his arm. He blushes as they smother him in kisses.

'Mickey,' they shout, 'you look dead sexy in that cardi.' Colette ruffles his hair affectionately.

'Coming to the booth later when I DJ?' he asks. 'I'll play

some Infant Cosmopolitan.'

'Infant Cosmopolitan, what the funk is that?' Ruby asks, over her mobile.

'It's me band,' Collette replies, 'it's the band am singing with.'

Ruby tries to stifle a laugh.

'It'll light up the dance floor I reckon.' Mickey says.

'That's not you singing on it.' Ruby says to Colette, smiling but not meeting her eye.

'It bloody is. That's my singin' voice!'

'You sound like Pete Burns.'

'Er I sound like Debbie Harry mate.'

'You are not in a band Colette, that is a total lie.'

'See you in a bit then Mickey' Colette announces, ignoring her, then slapping Ruby on the arm when he moves away.

'Why do you have to come out with that?' she whispers, curling her arm through Ruby's.

'Well you're not singing in that band.'

'I will be soon - he don't know. I reckon he'll sort us out a record deal one day.'

'Does he know you work a thirty five hour week at Deirdre's Cut and Curl?'

'Does he shite.'

Colette checks to see if the DJ is watching her move across his field of vision. She wonders if the night will end with them sleeping together again now his fiancée is back in Cameroon.

Bright pink cocktails in hands, the girl in leopard print tailing behind them like a foot soldier, The Queens carve purposefully round the club, though they never seem to arrive anywhere.

As the evening peaks Colette's stare becomes more glazed, less icy; sometimes she goes twenty minutes without glancing in the mirror. She begins to dance as if she's forgotten herself. Ruby suddenly crushes her tube of lip-gloss with a drunken heel, and when Colette looks over she recognizes the look of hidden desperation in her friend's eyes. She wonders if Ruby's about to burst into tears. The girl in leopard print is dancing vivaciously with Roz on the dance floor, a host of boys surrounding them. Colette looks over scornfully, resentful that as the evening progresses their hierarchy becomes less absolute.

'Some people have no respect' she murmurs, to no one in particular. When her favorite song comes on she looks more bitter than ever, as if she has suddenly felt the gap between her self-perception and the usual outcomes her evenings have.

As closing time nears her and Ruby cluster in the stairwell, both waiting for one boy in particular to come and find them. They text in silence, each barely meeting the eye of the other. Colette looks up as the DJ plays the last track of the night, noting sadly that it isn't her song. As she sees the dark rectangle of night at the top of the stairs, suddenly the night outside seems more vaulting than ever. Something makes her reluctant to move back into that darkness again. It suddenly seems paramount that she goes back inside to the club to reaffirm her presence. But people have drunk too much, danced too much. Now she's just a girl in a complicated outfit, wearing too much eye makeup, with a resigned expression on her face.

'Is that Irish boy meeting you then?' Colette asks her. Ruby looks blankly up at her, but doesn't say a word.

'Are you meeting the DJ later?' she asks back.

'That pin prick? Nah, screw him' Colette says.

They linger a little longer at the foot of the stairs, Ruby still texting. Colette realizes she now has to go out into that night, as the music below fades. The lights are coming on in the club.

As the two girls step reluctantly up the stairs to that square of black above them, they walk more carefully than ever. Neither of them notice the trail of silver glitter they leave in their wake as they walk slowly into the world outside.

Jason Williams

Under Jason's cold, sarcastic exterior beats a miserable and twisted heart, hate filled and bitter at the world. His day job as an accountant fills him with the kind of self-loathing only hookers, crack addicts and traffic wardens can truly understand. His writing is not so much an escape, as a reflection of the personal hell he has created. He also enjoys line dancing and keep fit.

Meeting Joe

My name is Joe Fraizer, and I am an alcoholic.

I don't know exactly how it happened. I certainly never set out to become one.

Nobody ever does.

I guess I started out as what you might call a social drinker. Nights out, parties, whatever. Soon I was drinking to help deal with the stress of work. A glass of wine, a bottle of suds. Helps you to wind down after a hard day at the office. Before long I'd use any excuse just to have a drink. That's all an alcoholic needs, you see. Excuse and opportunity.

And believe me, there's always an excuse if you're prepared to look hard enough.

For me the opportunity comes with the job. I work as a local bar tender. Plenty of people preach to me about my job, questioning how I ever expect to stay sober working in this place. The answer is always the same. I need the money. It's all well and good taking the moral high ground, but I've got bills to pay same as everybody else. Finding work in this town is never easy, particularly with an addiction.

I've been sober for twenty three days now, but like any alcoholic will tell you, I don't feel clean. The truth is you never feel truly clean. Once an alcoholic, you're an alcoholic for life. Don't believe all the wash powder commercials you see on TV. There are some stains you can never truly be rid of.

To be surrounded by the stuff day after day is like a constant hell on earth. Every shift is both physically and mentally draining, to the point of sheer exhaustion. I still get the shakes in my hands, and bouts of nausea hit without warning. I have trouble holding down solid food, my stomach rebelling against anything remotely wholesome. The lack of sustenance has left me lethargic and weak, and I suffer from dizziness and headaches as a result.

The nights are by far the worst though, when I'm left on my own and the doubts begin to crawl from the shadows. Most nights I can't sleep, and sit up until the early hours watching reruns of Cheers. I sometimes think if I just have a small drink, just a tiny night cap, it would get me off. Even as I think of it I know the dangers, yet the thought slowly burrows its way into my subconscious, whispering to me like an old friend, offering the ever-tempting route of escape. Every hour that passes becomes harder, the urge growing stronger. Sometimes the flat walls feel like a prison, the tiny room unbearable and oppressive. Usually I go for a walk, hoping the air and the open space might do me some good.

It doesn't.

Nothing can help me when I get to this stage. Nothing but the drink. These are the demons I've created. I sold my soul for vodka, and they're taking it back in instalments.

When I do sleep I have nightmares, and often wake sweat drenched and shaking. The images are often vivid and terrifying, and I struggle to piece any sense of coherency to them.

My one salvation, my hope in the nightmare that is my life, is my sponsor Tony. This man has been the greatest of inspirations to me since I started the programme. I needed help. I need help. I know that. I've known it for years, but was too damn stubborn and too damn ashamed to admit it, to myself as much as anybody. You'll hear plenty of alcoholics mention the first step to recovery is admitting you have a problem. Let me set the record straight right here and now. Most of us know what we are. You can't hide from it, no matter how much you pretend. In the darkest places, when you're alone and afraid, you know what you are, what you've become. Admitting it to others might make you feel better, but even with the mask in place, you know. The difficult thing has always been caring enough to do something about it.

Tony is a real hard case. The man has been there and done it.

He's been through the pain, the lies. The despair. Somehow he came out the other side. He doesn't flower you with positivity. No point in sugaring the pill. He tells it exactly how it is; the hardest, most soul destroying experience a person can ever undertake.

Tony is in his seventies, and he's been sober for over forty years. He's still an alcoholic, and you won't ever hear him deny it.

I'll never forget the first words he ever spoke to me.

'Few people ever get clean, and most who try don't succeed. You can't do it for friends, you can't do it for your family. Sometimes, when a building is beyond saving, there's no point in plastering up the cracks. You need to rip it down. If it isn't destroyed completely, no point in trying to rebuild it'.

'The question is son, how much have you left to destroy?'

I'd never spoken to the man before. He just walked over as calm as you like and asked me the question. For several heartbeats I stood there, unsure if I was expected to respond. The foam cup in my hand began to shake, spilling cheap, bitter coffee across my jeans. Tony just stood there waiting, his eyes cold and unmoving.

Never has another person had such an impact upon me. To this day I don't know why he did it, why he chose me in particular, but since then he's been like a father. I feel like I owe every one of my twenty three drink free days to him. No matter how bad things get, no matter how low I've fallen, he always seems able to drag me back up. He doesn't massage my ego or go easy on me. He's old school. He tells me when I'm being a jerk, when I'm feeling sorry for myself. That's what I really respect about him.

Tonight the bar's empty. Just a handful of regulars sat nursing their beers, most avoiding the wife, a few trying to find the next one.

I get the usual comments made about my name; 'Hey, Joe Fraizer. Like the boxer right?'

I just smile and nod politely. 'Yeh, like the boxer.'

I glance briefly over at the clock on the far wall - 23.40.

Only twenty minutes till closing time. Once again the thought fills me with a certain apprehension. Twenty minutes till I'm forced back home, back to the isolation, the mind-numbing boredom. In an effort to keep myself occupied I'm suddenly aware of a million things that need doing. The bar top, perfectly clean only minutes earlier, could now do with a second wipe. Bowls of nuts are carefully removed from the bar, to be stored neatly in the cupboard in the back.

Even as I launch myself into my new found duties a fresh face stumbles through the door. For a moment only my interest flickers, until the silhouetted figure moves into the light, his face once again recognisable.

'Hey there Joey lad,' Gerry slurs incoherently, stumbling forward and landing heavily across the bar

Gerry-the-fucking-paddy-O'Riley. A failure of the same programme I'm enrolled onto. A living testament to the fact the system doesn't always work.

'Hit me with a Whiskey Sour Joey, me old mate,' he grins, swaying dangerously on the bar stool as he fumbles in his pocket for a lighter.

I find myself shrugging disinterestedly, reaching for the bottle and pouring out a healthy measure. Some would think I'm a heartless bastard, but if he doesn't get it here, he'll get it elsewhere. It's his choice to do something about it. It's his problem, not mine. Who am I to suddenly be the judge of all men?

Gerry grasps the glass tightly, his trembling hand steadying as he clutches the precious liquid.

'Guess you heard about the old timer then,' he mutters absently, cocking back his head and downing the contents in a single swallow.

'What old timer?' I sigh. It's getting late, and I'm in little mood for drunken chitter-chatter.

'That Tony from rehab. Gone and had himself a stroke or something. Thought that tough old bastard would live forever.'

The words hit me like a steam train, my breath catching suddenly in my throat. For several seconds I can't speak, my chest tight, my breathing desperate and ragged.

'Is he ok?' I manage finally. I watch in wide-eyed horror as the drunk before me begins to chuckle.

'Ok? He's dead mate. Fucking dead. Any chance of another?'

The final words are lost on me as the news pierces my subconscious.

Dead.

I feel like the world has just collapsed around me. Tears are welling in my eyes, and I make little effort to fight them back. Angrily my fists clench and unclench, my knuckles white, my frustration insatiable. Ignoring the drunk before me I reach for a bottle, pouring myself a large Scotch. I need a drink.

Oh fuck how I need a drink right now.

I raise the glass nervously to my lips, my hands shaking violently, my palms sweating.

For a moment I find myself hesitating, staring through tear filled eyes to the depths of the liquid before me. I can barely hold back the choking anger, the despair, as I picture the old man's face once more. Suddenly I'm more unsure than ever. Every emotion, every sinew within me, is struggling for dominance.

What would Tony say if he was here?

The thought rises from the raging depths of my emotion, like a dying light in the turmoil of darkness. A tiny, fragile beacon, whispering words of salvation, yet so easily extinguished. If I do this now, there's no going back. No escape, no redemption. No hope. For only a moment I hesitate.

With a shaking hand I raise the glass to my lips, and damn myself once more.

All you ever need is an excuse.

My name is Joe Fraizer, and I am an alcoholic.

Philip Clark

Phil was born in Leicester but don't hold that against him. He's been trying to string together a coherent paragraph for years but still regularly falls short, however some publications have chosen to humour him by featuring his work, including Fissure Magazine, Clockwise Cat and Poetic Diversity. He lives in Salford and is working on a novel.

The Method

I had ensured that all vital areas of my scrawny carcass had been washed for my pending night out in town. It had been a fairly bog-standard day, nothing too much to write home about, but it hadn't bothered me because I was stepping out that night to meet a girl I had exchanged phone numbers with some weeks ago.

I had been thinking incessantly about the nature of twenty first century young love, it all appeared quite repulsive, non-descript and pointless to me. I hadn't endured the necessity of real female companionship for some time; in fact I was kind of out of practice. When I considered further, young love and my fairly arid sex life then I related it more to behaviour and character, my character.

What I'm getting at is this, when I look around and consider the relationships most of my female friends have with their boyfriends, there never seems to be any redeeming features, there never seems to be any enjoyment, it always seems more like an endurance test. A lot of the time their boyfriends are arseholes, but they just keep plodding on sustaining a relationship for years. I ask them what they like about their boyfriends and they just stare at me, open mouthed, stumped.

'Are they intelligent?' I ask.

'Are they shit hot in the sack?'

'Have they got a fucking massive dick?'

'Do they treat you amazing?'

Still open mouthed, still no answer.

And what I find even more vexing is that I have all these qualities and I can't get any action for love or money. So I decided that night to adopt a pretty shallow, sure fire method, one that'd probably secure me a bit of action. I left the complex and headed right onto Regent Road towards the city. The dark blue and fiery orange hue of the midsummer urban chaos was beginning to cover me from all sides as I passed the plastic eatery of the Harry Ramsden's restaurant.

The girl in question, Lisa, lived in Castlefield with her brother, although we'd decided to meet in a subterranean joint called Corbiers, just off Deansgate on the northern flank of town. I followed the chicane of the road around onto Liverpool Street, passing the Cask bar.

I turned left onto Deansgate and continued up; the animals, the pork chops and the gristle of Saturday night street life already buzzing around in flock, though disguised in white shirts and black trousers. I continued floating, passed the Great Northern and felt the sharp point of Bar 38's shard like exterior in the corner of my eye. I swung a right and descended the dank yellowy staircase of Corbiers. I had arrived.

The bar was reasonably full; it felt hot and humid as if the uncontrollable perspiration of a working week was filling every cubic inch of this tight underground womb. I spotted Lisa, she spotted me and waved, and I raised my eyebrows and turned towards the bar and ordered a drink: just one for myself. There, it's easy being an arsehole, it's easy being a twat. I took my drink over and sat with Lisa.

'Hi,' she said, 'You're late,' a soppy smirk covering her beautiful face.

I glanced up at her, straight faced, 'Well, good things come to those who wait Lisa.'

There it's easy being an arsehole, It's easy being obnoxious.

During our conversation in the underground dwelling I spoke only about me, I didn't ask her anything about her life or her friends or anything. It's easy being arrogant.

We finished our drinks and I suggested moving back down the other end of Deansgate, though not too far because I didn't want to give the game away just yet. I suggested Bar 38. She agreed. She was sweet but fuck it. We hurried passed the early evening glass exterior of the bar, all bouncers and boredom; we entered and manoeuvred ourselves towards the bar.

'It's your round,' I said.

She looked up at me, confused, slightly deflated, as if she felt under appreciated.

'Oh ok,' she said, 'what do you want?'

I deliberately looked around and blatantly looked up and down a fit blonde who was stood next to her.

'Beer.' I barked. It's easy being lecherous.

We sat and drank our drinks, Lisa looked uneasy; I was merely grinning and moving my head in time to the music and the rhythm of the fit blonde girl dancing in front of the bar. We finished our drinks and I suggested going to Cask bar on Liverpool Street. She agreed and we left. I was fairly satisfied that the method was beginning to pay its dividends.

We entered Cask; I had near on fifty sheets in my back pocket, though pretended to be skint nonethelessso she'd buy me another beer. It's easy being tight.

She agreed and we sat down, at that point saying very little, she got her phone out of her hand bag.

'Who are you texting?' I asked.

'Oh just my brother, he worries about me.'

'I bet it's nice to know somebody cares.'

She looked at me, and then she looked down at the table. A pang of guilt hit me, I felt shit, I wanted to tell her how beautiful I thought she looked or something to that effect but I refrained, and I decided to stick with my original plan.

We finished our drinks and outside on the street I suggested something to eat at Harry Ramsden's. You see the trick was I remembered all these places I had passed on the way to meet her and figured that by doing the same row of bars but in reverse it would pretty much lead us to my flat, and hence convenience or something of the like would mean she'd come back and let me fuck her. It's easy being shallow.

Conflicting testimony ensued, she had other ideas.

'No,' she said, 'let's go to Dukes in Castlefield. It's only around the corner. My brother's in there. I'd like you to meet him.'

I hesitated, 'Err, yeah, err, OK then.' Shit, I thought, the method had been thwarted at the final hurdle.

We entered Dukes and approached the bar; her brother was stood there waiting for us on his own. He was fairly stocky with a tuft of blonde hair. She hugged her brother, turned to me and informed me she was going to sit down. Her brother looked at me.

'Lisa texted me earlier,' he said, 'she told me you were treating her like shit.' My head sank, then I met his gaze and winked.

'Well you know mate, lads will be lads.'

He looked at me and shook his head, smiling, as if however fraudulent we were on the same wavelength. Then he socked me a good one on the cheek and I fell to the floor. The right side of my face felt numb. Lisa approached me, looming over my pathetic body.

'You prick, I thought you were different,' she said.

They both left. I stood up and left too. On the way home I felt bad, I felt wholeheartedly like I had deserved that punch in the face, but nonetheless I felt equally as bad that I'd have to go home to chicken fried rice and soft core voyeurism.

Deflated and ashamed I pontificated: fair play I had acted totally out of character that night, but then again maybe that just proves that in reality we're all just a bunch of arseholes.

It does seem to be an ever redeeming human characteristic, however, it's evidently not so easy to avoid behaving like an arse.

Tom Arnold

Tom lives in Chester with a one year old puke machine, three year old mini-beserker and his lovely Irish wife. He mainly visits the zoo in his spare time and changes nappies. In the remaining three seconds left after the puke monsters go to bed - he writes and recently completed his fourth novel.

The Morning After

It's a fact that most people die on a Monday. Mondays suck. Monday - if it were a person would have no friends. Monday also has a huge chip on it's shoulder. Everyone hates it. Even my mum - and my mum practically loves everything.

So it was no surprise when Monday hit me with a sucker-punch to the fuzznuts at 06:58.

I rolled over in bed and wrapped my arm around the fat but highly attractive girl in the bed next to me. She had a name - but I chose not to remember it. In my head she was "fat but beer goggly stunning girl from that house party last night." She was butt naked, as was I and we had had glorious fat and sweaty sex for a large part of Sunday night. It had been a lager, vodka, red-bull fuelled night of massive excess. But when you're a student that's kinda what's expected.

Bruuuuurpppppppp!!!

I farted at the same time as I rubbed my aching head. The hazy phrase 'never again' was beginning to form in wispy red letters in front of my eyes. Somewhere an inch above them a small pixie-sized man had unscrewed the top of my skull and begun an ambitious fishing expedition using a seven inch ice pick and a rubber hammer as a rod. Pink flesh shrunk back in fear and pulsed in horror.

Despite the early stages of alcohol trauma setting in - a rogue part of my anatomy was putting up a resilient last gasp defence. If this pixie was gonna drill my brain dry - then I was gonna at least die happy.

I sent out test signals to my hot, rotund date. 'You up for it?' I suggested.

I was making myself sick - was this shag gluttony? Was it beer sloth? What kind of sin was this? There was no, absolutely not one, excuse for sober Monday morning fat sex two hours before my first economics lecture...or was there?

I hated myself. What had I become?

We were spooning. The classic shag slumber pose. I rubbed my hand against her firm thigh. And up, tickling, tickle wickle, tickle wickle towards the glory mound.

'That's weird,' I thought. 'That's really weird. What the fu...?'

It's difficult to convey the feeling of shit-me-up terror that swamped me at 06.59. It reminded me of the intense shame and horror that used to wash over me (literally) every time I pissed my pants at primary school (I did that a lot. Much to Miss Trully's vexation). That feeling of being caught in a terrible act, a shameful act. A taboo. Animals piss and shit on themselves. Pigs and cows - not us.

I rushed my hand over her fat, sun-deprived, wobble tummy and up towards her chest - waiting for the rise. And fall. I had to make sure. I had to. My dick was already ahead of the game. Gone back up practically inside my crotch like a terrapin snappin' it's head back into it's shell.

'Shit,' I croaked as I pushed back and rolled away instinctively. Back, back as far as I could get. Into next year - into the next galaxy. Back and over onto the floor with a thud and scrabbling for air and feeling my eyeballs melt into my head and the world turn red like someone let a grenade off inside my gut.

'Hurghhh hurgghhhh,' here came the waterfall. A vomit path of terror. 'Hurghhhh..' over the brown paisley carpet and up against the walls. Spitter spatter spitter spatter - does it really matter?

'She's dead. She's only gone and got fucking dead!' I murmured to no-one in particular as I lay all foetus-like on the floor. Bathed in last night's dinner - kebab and chips.

I lay on the floor dry-wretching for ten maybe fifteen minutes. Composing myself. Eventually, the overpowering stench of my stomach contents and perhaps even the imperceptible initial whiff of a body on the turn forced me into action.

Slowly, slowly. With fear in my heart and horror in my head. Slowly, I hauled my sorry arse back up onto the bed and leant over the fat girl's body. God I wished she had a name now. Fat Dead Girl had a distinctively disrespectful ring about it. I thought about her mum and her dad. How sad they'd be. Their baby girl all dead. So sordid, so so wrong.

I rolled her over onto her back and gulped. Sweat trickled down my nose and dripped onto her chest. She had little wisps of fine black downy hair over her breasts and wobbly tummy. I stared at them intently, lost for a second in a train of thought. My Star Wars pillow covered her face. Kinda like someone smothered her. Hmmm...curiouser and curiouser.

I flipped the pillow off of her. Looked at her face good and proper. Bile rose up like a geyser in my throat. Her mouth was open. Nothing wrong there you'd think. 'Cept of course she was dead - and her mouth was wedged. Wedged with a size twenty pair of M & S black knickers. This was not a good sign. This was a distinctly certain sign that I was gonna spend the next fifty years of my life on the sex offenders list being hounded by the News of the World if I ever got out of the maximum security prison for sickos.

'I definitely don't remember that.' Monday morning showstopper would have been an understatement.

Why would she stick a pair - presumably her pair - of size twenty knickers in her mouth and kill herself?

Boy was I slow that morning. Finally, finally as I lay on the bed next to her - post post coital. It dawned on me. I racked my brains for a memory. Nothing - nada - zip - diddly. There had to be a logical explanation.

'Oh my God. No. Why? It must have been me. I bloody killed her - I must have fucking killed her in her sleep.

It made no sense though. I'd never thought about killing anyone before. Not even once. Why kill someone when you can shag them? Oh my god - unless that was my sick drunken plan? Was this how necrophiliacs started? They all had to start somewhere. Why not today for me? Noooooooo. Surely there were signs - warning signals. Unhealthy interest in Zombie movies and a fixation for vampires in bondage kit?

'Doof Doof.' I froze. It was my door.
'Just a minute.' I yelled.
'Johnny. Let me in. It's me.'
And it was. Bettina, my beautiful Swedish girlfriend was at the door.

'Open the door honey. Let me in. Come on honey - we're late.'

'Shitbox.' I stammered. This was bad. Should I just open the door and be done? Admit the truth?

'Hey sweetie - I got smashed last night, pulled a fat bird, brought her back home, stuck a pair of knickers in her gob and banged her to death. Could you call the police please darling. Bruckrupppppp!' (The Bruckurp bit would be my planning ahead for the inevitable court case. No-one would convict me of murder if I clucked like a randy chicken. Insanity was my only sane option. Surely my only option.)

Or was it?

I had to think quick. The wolves were circling.

'Open up Johnny.' There was a hint of threat in there now. A sixth sense had been triggered and the missus was on to something.

'I'm...er...I'm just getting dressed,' I stuttered.

The door handle rattled. She wanted in. Thank God I'd had the foresight to cheat on my long term girlfriend with the door locked to my bedroom. One point to me. Shoot me in the head and remove my nutsack for being stupid enough to wake up with the girl I just cheated with dead in the bed next to me. Two points to the God of embarrassing situations. If it got much worse he'd be calling his omnipotent buddy The God of excruciatingingly painful deaths at the hands of a demented girlfriend-armed with only a sandal and some chewing gum.

'Open the goddamned door now.' she was losing it. Rapidly.

'Think Johnny, think.'

This was make or break time. There was so much I wanted to do with life. So much. And I knew I didn't do it. It wasn't in me. Killing? Killing like that? I gulped and made a decision. It was wrong. So wrong. But I needed to buy some time. Save my life.

Shakily. Shakier than Shakin' Stevens in an earthquake - shakily I got to my feet and grabbed the bed sheet and slung it over the dead girl. I noticed an oozing of blood begin to seep through the white sheets where it touched her head. Was she bleeding out of her mouth? Her eyeballs? Her earholes now? Is that what dead bodies did? This was all new territory for me - they never taught this in kindergarten. I dabbed at the blood as it seeped through the sheet from dead fat girl.

'Jesus. I need to give her a name. I can't just call her dead fat girl forever. Mary. Ok. Mary it is then. Come on Mary - we're going on a little journey.'

I sighed as I wrapped the sheet all the way over her. I almost caught myself worrying that I'd suffocate her with the sheet stretched so tight over her bloodied knicker-stuffed face.

'Heave...' I strained as I tried to lift her.

'For the love of God...' I groaned as I tried to get leverage under her armpits. It was no use. She had been a big girl. BIG. And in death - gravity was even more unforgiving.

'Bang Bang Bang BANG.' the door was beginning to rattle on it's hinges now.

'Shitbox.' I said again as I laboured with my dead body - with Mary. There was nothing for it. I clambered over her into the spoon position again.

'Sorry,' I whispered roughly where I thought her ear was and then shoved her straight off the bed onto the floor. I heard some floorboards splinter and my heart raced out of control.

I jumped out the bed, onto the floor and began to roll her straight under the bed. Down amongst the old sneakers, used condoms and girlie mags. I felt a great pang of guilt for my act. But also acknowledged that my fear of going to jail greatly out-weighed that guilt. What did that make me? Even if I were not the killer - I was a morally sick individual. I deserved to go to jail for that alone. Did I not?

Mary fitted snug under the bed. I slung her clothes right under there with her and launched my footie kit on top. I looked back at my improvised murder scene clean up and wondered if it passed muster.

'Fuckbucket.' I groaned when I looked at the bed.

There was a giant dent where Mary had slept. You could get that past a bloke - but a spot like that was bread and butter to a girlfriend trained in the art of unfaithfulness detection.

I grabbed my laptop from the corner of the room and a bundle of library books and scattered them over the dent. I then scrambled for the door.

'Bettina babe...' I smiled and took a right hook to the eyeball as she brushed me aside. She studied the room intently before turning to me and delivering the coup de grace. I took the kick to the nuts like a man and duly crumpled to the floor.

It was as I lay in silent agony on the carpet - alone once more - that I noticed the cigarette in the ashtray with the red lipstick smothered all over it. Damn. My cover was blown.

'Mondays - I bloody hate Mondays.' I grumbled as I began to douse the bedroom in lighter fuel from my Zippo and lit the match. I closed the door and headed for the station. To a new life - a life of wild abandonment and living on the run.

Did I mention that Mondays really really suck?

Blaine Ward

He's a funny one is wor Blaine.
His home (a tiny mahogany box lined with blue velvet) bears a brass plate with the inscription "*Here lives an overfat flatulent windbag;a master of inconsequence masquerading as a guru.*"
Oh, and Blaine Ward isn't his real name!

<u>An Eye for an Eye</u>

As I struck him hard across the left temple with the monkey wrench I felt nothing.

Nothing, that is, aside from the force of the blow reverberating along the muscles in my forearms. No remorse, no pity. Not even any sadness. No joy, no pleasure. Nothing. Glancing over my shoulder, I noticed that blood had begun to surround the body as a raspberry compote might surround a plump, milky-white blancmange.

I placed the wrench on the cement floor of the cell, reached for the green plastic container and poured its contents over the prone body. The smell of petrol made my eyes water. The Original Cook's safety matches (complete with wipe clean box) were on the small Formica table. Having adjusted my safety goggles, I pulled the mask over my mouth as I struck the first match, flicked it towards the soaked mass on the floor and stood back as the clothed body ignited, making the same noise as the gas boiler in our house when the central heating kicks in. Despite the heat, I shivered as I remembered how, as a boy, I had been fascinated by the burning of the Guy Fawkes effigy on November the fifth. I had already taken the precaution of fitting my earplugs in place so at least I was spared the screaming. I hated the screaming. Some colleagues fitted noseplugs too but I didn't mind the smell. It reminded me of summer barbecues. When the puddle of blood caught fire it coagulated then sizzled like black pudding in the Sunday breakfast frying pan.

Of course, at that time I had no knowledge of the tenor of his defence. They never divulged such information to me. They said it was to ensure I remained objective. So I didn't get emotionally involved, they said. I could see their point. But truth will out. We read that at school. The Merchant of Venice. "And you will know the truth, and the truth will make you free."

That's from the Bible. The old Bible, I mean. You know, before the the changes. The Gospel of Saint John.

Later, there would be a lot of argument between the lawyers and the judges about the interpretation of words in books. Books and statutes and contracts.

"The devil can cite scripture for his own purpose."

That's The Merchant of Venice too. I would do a lot of reading while I waited for my fate to be determined. A lot of Shakespeare and quite a bit of historical, comparative religion. Strange how the thought of imminent death might come to influence your choice of reading material.

But for now, it was all congratulatory back slapping and hints about promotion and 'you're one of us now, son' from the boss. Then it started. That reporter on the television banging on about how crucial evidence had been ignored or - worse still - deliberately suppressed by the Crown Prosecution Service. Then the twin brother going public with his story about how he had already confessed to the murder but had been dismissed by the police on the basis he was trying to save his brother's neck or - worse still - to concoct a technical defence whereby they would both escape justice. It all got a bit too complex for me and I don't mind admitting I didn't really understand what they were talking about half the time. What I do know is that there were legal challenges by both prosecution and defence and that both sides quoted at length from the Bible and various other legal and religious tracts.

That was the thing about the Bible, I thought. For every argument there was an equal and opposite argument. Take this job of mine for instance. I was brought up to believe in the primacy of The Ten Commandments. Thou shalt not kill and all that. My morals weren't merely shaped on the anvil of the Old Testament either. Oh no. Young Jesus got a fair look in too. Turn the other cheek and all that quasi-gay stuff. But then I remembered the good old principle of retributive justice: An eye for an eye and all that. Now that little beauty featured in no fewer than three books of the Bible (Exodus, Leviticus and Deuteronomy if you are interested) so it must really be a Holy Trinity, right? Right?

Anyway, when Cameron got in and pushed his Retributive

Justice Bill through Parliament the ads shot up everywhere. The Lex Talionis campaign alone must have cost millions. You remember it don't you? Of course you do. Who could forget it? Those pictures. Made my stomach turn if you want to know the truth. It was a master-stroke getting the Pope onside though. And that summit meeting when the first drafts of the combined Talmud/Bible/Quran were agreed was an act of multicultural diplomacy bordering on genius. Granted, the initial working title of this particular Holy Trinity ("The Talbiran") was a political foot-shooter of biblical proportions but the spin doctors got in quick to repair the damage and the latest title ("The Biqurmud" or "Bykermud" in the revised St James's version) at least has the merit of lacking the obvious connotations of the first.

It had all started for me when I got laid off at the abattoir. The girl at the Job Centre had suggested I should apply. She said I had "relevant experience" and pointed out that the terms and conditions of employment were unparalleled. She was particularly effusive about the non-contributory pension scheme (which would be tax free) and reassured me that in the event of any conflict of interest I would be automatically switched to another case. Of course, the training course would be no picnic but she felt I would stand a good chance of at least being short-listed for a local post.

I sailed through the preliminaries, passed the aptitude tests with flying colours and was then long-listed for the induction training. This proved to be no problem for me either, but to be honest it bore little relevance to the job I was eventually given as a trainee Retribution Executive Officer (REO). I started off observing several "retribution operations", before progressing to assisting.

Eventually, I was carrying out my own executive operations (the word "executions" was strictly off limits) without assistance and whilst I wouldn't exactly say I enjoyed the work, I didn't really mind it either. It wasn't my job to decide who was guilty or not guilty. I simply had to carry out the decision made by the court. It was hardly different from the function of a court bailiff, except that I was dealing in lives, not second hand furniture.

The first few ops were a little tricky but once you got the hang of it (no pun intended), there was nothing to it. And the pay...oh boy! The pay was much better than it had been at the slaughter house. Admittedly, I didn't get any free samples or off-cuts to bring home but to tell you the truth I had become a virtual vegetarian after having worked in the abattoir all those years so the perks weren't really much of a miss. With all the extra money I was bringing in we were able to move to a bigger house in the country and I even bought three little pigs as pets. Tony, Gordon and Peter we called them. Deep down I think the act of buying the piglets felt like some kind of atonement for my past sins. As they frolicked around their pen they put me in mind of the pink link sausages that hung in the butcher's window.

Of course, every job has its horror stories and this one was no exception. My mate Dick (name changed in accordance with statutory instrument SI 499 of 2013) really drew the short straw one day when he was assigned to a particularly nasty indirect operation that had the added difficulty of having attracted a lot of media interest.

"Inops" as we called them were often perceived as the worst kind because there was a feeling abroad in the office that it was not really fair that a perpetrator should be punished in this way. Not that anyone would dare say so in public.

You look a little confused and that's not altogether surprising. Let me explain. After the Retributive Justice Bill received the Royal Assent and became a fully fledged Act of Parliament (known on the inside and then more widely as "i4i") not only was it passed retrospectively (meaning that those in custody awaiting sentence could be subjected to the death penalty even though this had not been on the horizon when they were convicted - which I must admit does seem a little harsh) but the concept of the inops - which had been hidden away in the small print - came to the fore with a vengeance.

Rather than go into all the technical issues, permit me to

illustrate the point by telling you what happened with Dick's case. A pervert had killed a six year old girl out in Norfolk somewhere (place name changed in accordance with statutory instrument SI 500 of 2013). He had sexually assaulted her too but I will spare you the details. The thing was that this paedophile had covered his own tracks by carrying on what appeared to be a normal life. He was a Religious Studies teacher for God's sake. He also had a wife and two children. A boy of nine and a girl of seven. So Dick was assigned the case and was initially quite pleased about this. I recall him saying that he would take great pleasure in ridding society of another Gary Glitter. But he hadn't read the small print. That wasn't how i4i worked. You see, the retribution for the taking of a child's life was the taking of the same in return. The victim's family had the option to invoke clause 17B if they wished (whereby the murderer could be dispatched in substitution) but they were understandably too distressed to make any decision so by default Dick had to perform the operation on the murderer's seven year old daughter. The murderer tried to overturn the decision on appeal but to no avail. The i4i concept was clear and in the absence of any option being taken up by the victim's family the like for like clause applied.

The murder itself had been especially gruesome (I will spare you the details) so what had started as elation for Dick ended up as a real traumatic experience for him. Credit where credit is due, he did his duty but he was never the same man again. In fact , after a lengthy period of sick leave he ended up taking early retirement and going to live in Dorset (place name again changed in accordance with statutory instrument SI 500 of 2013).

"The large print giveth and the small print taketh away."

That's Tom Waits. As you will soon find out, as well as reading, I would also get the chance to listen to a lot of music whilst awaiting my destiny.

So to get back to the main story, after much legal to-ing and fro-ing, it was decided that the conviction of the twin I had already operated on was "unsafe".

My first thought was: Unsafe for whom? After all, his behaviour had been pretty "unsafe" for the victim whose head he had smashed in with a monkey wrench before torching him down a back alley. So what if the DNA evidence suggested it was more likely to have been his twin brother who had committed the murder? Why not operate on him too, just to be on the safe side? But no, it wasn't that simple they said. Had I not read the small print in my contract they asked?

Cutting short a very long and tedious story, it turned out that there was no exemption clause or "hold safe" clause in my contract. I don't pretend to understand the legal niceties but the top and bottom of it was that as I may have operated on the wrong person so I was held personally liable. This meant that i4i applied to me too. My only hope was to seek clemency from the family of the wronged, which in this case meant the twin brother.

I know this is all a bit confusing so just to make sure you have grasped my predicament I will go over it again. I had carried out my duty, done as I was ordered to do and through no fault of my own it would appear I had operated on the wrong person. So now I was facing a retributive operation to satisfy the i4i law and my only hope of saving my own skin was to appeal to the twin brother who in all likelihood had committed the murder in the first place. What a mess!

I didn't feel too happy at the prospect of being extinguished I must admit, but I have my standards and there was no way I was going to kow-tow to that piece of filth. So, I tried to delay the inevitable as long as possible by pursuing the appeals process to the bitter end, but eventually my legal team told me that there was no more they could do for me so I spent my remaining period of pre-operative confinement enriching my mind by reading, listening to music and practising Hatha yoga.

From time to time someone would pass me the news that it was still possible that my sentence would be commuted to life imprisonment because the powers that be were apparently having great difficulty in recruiting a fellow executive to perform the operation on me. It seemed that many of my colleagues were fearful that the same fate might await them if it were to be subsequently determined that my operation had been illegal. They were seeking assurances that they would be granted full indemnity against honest mistake and that some form of "hold harmless" clause would be incorporated into the contract of employment before they would agree to operate on me. I could fully appreciate their concerns but frankly, after the initial surge of optimism had subsided, I had given up caring and lapsed into a state of resigned acceptance. In the absence of the highly unlikely scenario that any such changes would be retrospectively enacted they would come too late for me so I was quite content to mark time with my music, my reading and of course my yoga. I took the view that it was not so much a question of if, but when.

Despite my sense of resignation, it still came as something of a shock to the system when one morning I was told without ceremony that later that day my operation would go ahead. I suppose on a deeper level that old silver-tongued trickster Hope had been at work on my heart, but like all charlatans, having seduced me, he was to cast me aside.

It all happened so fast. I was led to the familiar operating theatre, seated at the solitary Formica table and awaited my nemesis. I must confess I was more than a little curious to find out who had been given the job but I guessed that I wouldn't know the person anyway because my own workmates would no doubt invoke the conflict of interest clause, so my executor (let's not be coy about it) would not be known to me.

I glanced around the room, at the box of safety matches on the table, the wrench leaning against the wall and the plastic container that I surmised must be holding the petrol. Then the door quietly opened and a vaguely familiar figure entered the room. He was clothed in the regulation overalls but - and this was a first - his face was covered by a black Balaclava helmet with small holes for his eyes and mouth. Had an agreement been reached with the government? I wondered.

As he shuffled past me I was almost certain that he whispered the single word 'Sorry' but before I had time to think further I was floored as the monkey wrench crashed into my temple. As I lay on the cold cement watching the purple blood leak from my ears, I recognised the outline of my operator. Good old Dick.

They must have coaxed him back out of retirement. At least I had the consolation of knowing that I would be dispatched by a pro. I knew too that he would feel nothing. Nothing at all. No sadness, no joy, no pleasure. Nothing aside from the reverberations along the muscles of his forearms as the wrench bit into my skull. A true pro.

I hope you read the small print this time Dick. And I hope you remembered to put your earplugs in.

Stephen Cooper

Stephen is currently inside the washing machine in his kitchen, because of a drunken New Years Eve bet, and wont be out again until spring.

Well, weather permitting anyway.

I Have Never Done That

I love sitting up here.

Up on the dormant ancient volcanic hill, I can see right over the mouth of the river and watch it escaping into freedom, into the sea. I wonder what it would be like to be a river?

Maybe the sea gets warmer when it is joined by this river, you know the way you feel when you have a piss in the sea and then it feels warm?

I have never done that.

I wonder is it an organised entry, or is it chaos down there at the core of the current?

I don't think it would be neat and organised.

I think it sort of swirls around and goes all over the place, fighting for breath, in a blind panic and frothing at the mouth like a fit, but then eventually, it sees it's safe and is welcomed into a new world, and settles down. Just like the way paint used to do in art class in school when you dipped your brush into the water to change the colour.I wonder where does the actual force which drives the river forward to release its silt and baggage from the land into that insatiable ocean come from?

That's why the river goes all swirly, a bit moody, I can see the dark mood from up here, it's like it's dying, because it knows it's coming to the end but then with a rush, it's climax and its rebirth in the next cycle is complete, as it is subsumed, and becomes part of something else. I think I understand.

I can see the whole estate from up here, it looks really neat, not like the rundown decaying mish mash of concrete and squalor I know it as. It's perhaps a bit naive of me to admit, but it's almost as if someone has sat and planned all this, all the roads and pavements and cul de sacs and where the street lamps go and where the different numbers and rows of houses begin and end.

Funny how my thoughts are so carefree and flitting up here, my mind is like a butterfly flying from thought to thought.

The wind blows on my face, it doesn't smell of anything, just nice fresh wind, makes me feel clean as if I have had a cleansing of any dark thought cobwebs from inside my head.

I like it up here, I am lying on my front, beside my American friend, on soft elephant grass, I don't know why it's called that, but I am comfortable with it, and on it.

I can see him getting into a car. The car looks tiny from here, but I know it's a BMW jeep, black of course; the houses are like the same size as in monopoly, except they aren't green.

Maybe he has had a row and is leaving his wife, maybe he won't come back.

No suitcase or luggage though, so maybe he is just going to the shop to buy something nice or he needs dog food for a dog he loves like the son he never had. Maybe he is going to go and pick up his bit on the side from work and take her for a drive and ride her up some secluded country lane. Or he could be going over to see a man who owns a chainsaw to borrow it and he will come back and cut into pieces the young boy who turned up earlier with his daughter and after being introduced, expressed an interest in how he would feel about imminently becoming a grandparent.

I hope I know where he is going.

The lights are still on in his house.

That means someone else is in there, or he wants to pretend that he is still there with a chainsaw, or a shotgun, or a baseball bat. Or maybe he left the lights on by mistake because his mind is on the next big deal, or problems with his staff under him, his working ants, his subordinates in his organisation. Maybe he is just going around to the shop and won't be more than two minutes, because he's lazy and can't be bothered to walk, or maybe it isn't even his car, and he's off to wherever he fucking wants.

Or maybe he is up to no good, as usual.

All round me there is life, look at these plants, my mind is off again, they are lucky, sitting up here, it's a great view, I look closely and notice not many have been picked, which is good, because I think they would miss each other if a few got picked by people and left the others all alone.

It would be, to them, like losing a member of the family to us, but then when the next shoot appears and blooms then that would be like an addition again to the family, like a birth, and everyone would be happy, until of course the next one from your family gets picked again eventually.

Now and then some bad plants have to be picked for the good of the rest though, some weeds strangle and entangle themselves around the good and innocent pretty flowers and they have to be picked out and removed. I suppose I feel the same about the bad plants in society, otherwise I wouldn't be up here with my American friend, would I?

It's only right, but I would never pick good plants.

I have never done that.

Loads of cars on that coast road. I can see their lights, and even I can tell the difference when they dip their headlights for the oncoming cars. I know a friend of mine who thinks it's dead funny to put his full beam on just as he is about to pass the other car, temporarily dazzling them.

I have never done that.

I can see the other town from here and the road linking it with this town, and there must be hundreds of lights, no thousands, hundreds and thousands. I remember them on my son's birthday cake each year.

I wonder how long I will have to wait tonight. This is my third night up here, I am getting to like it.

It gives you a sort of different perspective on things I think. All those people down there arguing about small irrelevant things; what channel to watch on TV, what song to listen to in their cars, drivers raging at the other ignorant bastard of a driver dazzling them with full beam as they whizz by, couples trapped in a house they can't afford to leave, men in marriages they can't afford to leave and the unemployed and sick who can barely afford to live, never mind even thinking about being able to leave.

I feel powerful in my job, especially when I am invisible to anyone else. I rest against my American friend, and lean my cheek against her, whilst I think about going home later and how long it will be until then.

I can see where the black BMW is going now, so I work my friend into action, I offer her all of it and she takes it, a snug fit, only half an inch in diameter, but hard as metal. The guy driving the Beamer is finally back at where we thought he would be, which is at the cache of weapons we have been watching for days, and it's also right in the cross hairs of my friend's sight.

They call him 'Pablo' and he likes to be called that, and he also likes to think he runs the show around here. It was Pablo who used my son as a drug dealer, and got him on heroin and who I blame for his subsequent overdose.

And my friend I was talking about earlier? She's a dependable American, a M107 .50 inch caliber long range sniper rifle; we are friends, and have been for a while now.

I am 1.546 kilometers away, but I can see 'Pablo' and his pock marked skin clearly as I breathe and watch the cross rise and fall on his face. I exhale for the last time and for a fraction of a second I share this action with 'Pablo', because he also exhales for the last time in this scene, and in that split second we are sharing as one the most important thing either of us will ever experience together.

My American friend senses this as I squeeze, and she buckles and spasms and ejaculates my seed with a shudder I feel right through my right shoulder down to my toes.

I exhale, again.

Now it's different, and it will never be the same as before, but then again with each passing second, life never is.

I am alone, and the brief connection is severed, literally.

Flicking the safety on with my thumb, I begin disassembling my American friend with care and methodical ease and place her back into her bed to rest with our spent casing, still lukewarm after discarding it's charge, straight and true.

As I pack up I see a pretty little flower, and I am just about to absent mindedly pick it, when I realise and stop.

I have never done that.

Industrial Strength Fiction

Visit us today at
www.bykerbooks.co.uk

On the site you can browse our books, read exclusive interviews with authors, check out the latest news from Britain's radgest underground press and read quality, FREE, short fiction from some of the country's up and coming authors.

NEWS	*Get the lowdown on all of our latest books and authors.*
COMPS	*Chances to win exclusive signed copies of top tomes.*
STORIES	*Read quality British fiction on the site...for nowt!*
BOOKS	*Browse our ever expanding catalogue of publications and ask yourself just how you ever managed without us.*

Come and have a look if you think you're hard enough!

Byker Books

Danny King

More Burglar Diaries

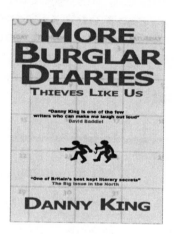

'One of Britain's best kept literary secrets'
The Big Issue in the North

Bex and Ollie are a couple of small-time burglars. They scratch a living robbing shops, burgling factories and emptying offices around the back-water town of Tatley.

Bex is the brains, Ollie drives the van.

Neither are particularly ambitious, preferring instead to think small and live comfortably, rather than aim high and risk time. The lads don't have it all their own way though; 'Weasel' of CID is only one faltering step behind them, the local criminal competition will do anything to stitch them up and the loves of their lives are wondering what the hell they've done to deserve them.

Things are about to finally catch up with Bex and Ollie.

www.bykerbooks.co.uk

Industrial Strength Fiction

Andy Rivers

I'm Rivelino - A Life of Two Halves

'funny, fanatical and thoroughly enjoyable'
Lovereading.co.uk

'When you consider them in a football sense you think of
'little Rotherham playing Newcastle? Oh the romance of the
cup.' Well all I could see was fifteen stone, pie eating nutters
covered in tattoos and no matter how much aftershave they'd
slapped on there'd be no fucking romance going on there I
can tell you...!'

Thanks to a family member taking him to his first match in the
early seventies whilst he was at an impressionable age Andy
Rivers discovered Newcastle United. Given the despair this
has caused him over the last thirty years it's fair to assume that
this action would be considered child abuse today. His story,
peppered with terrace wit and rough charm, will be identified
with by supporters everywhere.

www.bykerbooks.co.uk

Coming Soon...

Maxwell's Silver Hammer

After Billy Reeves had survived a poverty ridden and violent childhood on a council estate in Newcastle he thought he had it all; a loving family, money and respect but a face from the past with a point to prove and muscles to flex is out to bring his world crashing down on him.

After turning down the offer of a job with Tyneside's most paranoid and psychotic gang lord he's faced with bent police, a corrupt judge, an army of bouncers and the knowledge that if he makes one wrong move in this game of cat and mouse his family will end up imprisoned, abused or worse.

Billy is going to have to work very hard just to keep everyone he cares about alive and that means the gloves are coming off...

See next page for exclusive first look!

Maxwell's Silver Hammer

Prologue

Billy

He's waiting in the alley under the bridge for me; I spotted that big, pretentious Shogun of his by Kwiksave. It's a contradiction of visions that just sums the coke headed, muddled up prick quite nicely.

Vince Merry, believes himself to be the top man on Tyneside, my nemesis for so many years. He's had my little brother put away for murder and burnt down his business; threatened my ageing mother with violence; killed owld Dave and now he wants me. Well now he gets me, all of me.

I'm at the entrance to the alley under the bridge, there's only one streetlight and I'm under it, darkness and shadows all around me, the fine rain is visible against the light and the wind blows sweet wrappers around my feet. I feel in my jacket pocket for the knuckle-duster, its chunky, solid feel is reassuring. Sighing softly I look up into the Newcastle night sky for what could possibly be the last time and wonder how it ever came to this, thirty four years of keeping my head down and not offending the big boys, playing it safe and paying my dues every time and still, in the end, I have to fight it out with them. The streetlight is slightly comforting, it's got a warm yellow glow to it but it doesn't lift my mood, I would give anything to be cuddling up to Lisa now.

Growing up where and how I did I've always known that life's not fair, I constantly expect to have people shit on me, I accept this and probably deep down knew that one day it would come to this. I think I even half knew it would be with this wanker as well.

Weary and resigned to my fate I have to start this thing. I hope I finish it.

'Merry,' I call into the blackness. There's a rustling sound and two figures step forward into the half-light. Big Tony stands to the right of Merry, a tattooed behemoth, all broad shoulders, big neck and massive biceps, Merry himself is brandishing a big blade, again, I expected this.

My heart is pounding as the adrenalin rushes through my body, my legs feel frozen to the floor and my internal system is asking the question fight or flight?

Understandably my brain is screaming flight but my heart knows the score and is telling me that I must put this fucker to bed once and for all.

Looking at the knife,I go for the token question.

'Thought it was a straightener?'

He smiles at me without humour and replies, 'Grow up Billy, we're not at school any more.'

There's nothing more to say, it's time to start the endgame.

Putting my duster on my right fist I smile back and step into the alley towards them.

*   Released on 12/07/10   *

Available from selected book stores and all good online retailers.

'When it goes down you'd better be ready...'

Lightning Source UK Ltd.
Milton Keynes UK
23 July 2010
157402UK00001B/107/P